PINOCCHIO

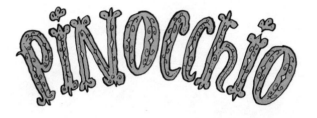

CARTOON CLASSICS

PINOCCHIO

retold by **KATE McMULLAN**

illustrated by **PASCAL LeMAITRE**

Christy Ottaviano Books

Henry Holt and Company

NEW YORK

Henry Holt and Company, LLC
Publishers since 1866
175 Fifth Avenue
New York, New York 10010
mackids.com

Henry Holt books may be purchased for business or promotional use. For information on
bulk purchases, please contact the Macmillan Corporate and Premium Sales Department
at (800) 221-7945 x5442 or by e-mail at specialmarkets@macmillan.com.

Library of Congress Cataloging-in-Publication Data
McMullan, Kate.
Pinocchio / retold by Kate McMullan ; illustrated by Pascal LeMaitre. — First edition.
pages cm. — (Cartoon classics)
Summary: A lonely woodcutter creates a puppet that comes to life,
but Pinocchio is more of a prankster than a pleasure until he learns that
being a real boy is much more complicated than simply having fun.
ISBN 978-0-8050-9699-6 (hardback)
1. Graphic novels. [1. Graphic novels. 2. Fairy tales. 3. Puppets—Fiction.] I. Lemaitre,
Pascal, illustrator. II. Title.
PZ7.7.M445Pin 2014   741.5'973—dc23   2014007036

First Edition—2014 / Designed by April Ward
The artist used pen-and-ink and colors enhanced by
Photoshop to create the illustrations for this book.

Printed in the United States of America by
R. R. Donnelley & Sons Company, Harrisonburg, Virginia
1 3 5 7 9 10 8 6 4 2

Dear readers,

Carlo Collodi is the pen name of an Italian author who wrote *Pinocchio* in the 1880s, and I've based this retelling on his charming story. Collodi's tale of the naughty puppet first appeared in a Roman newspaper, one short, suspenseful chapter at a time. Almost every chapter ended with a cliff-hanger that left readers thinking, "Surely this is the end of Pinocchio!" They had to wait a whole week to find out whether the feisty puppet lived or died. The newspaper stories became so popular that Collodi published them as a book, which has been loved by readers for more than a hundred years. And now we have Pinocchio's wild adventures, illustrated with great wit and style by Pascal Lemaitre in a graphic chapter book, offering readers a brand-new way to read this classic story.

For Gabriel Claudio Marzollo

—K. M.

For Lynn and Sam Waterston

—P. L.

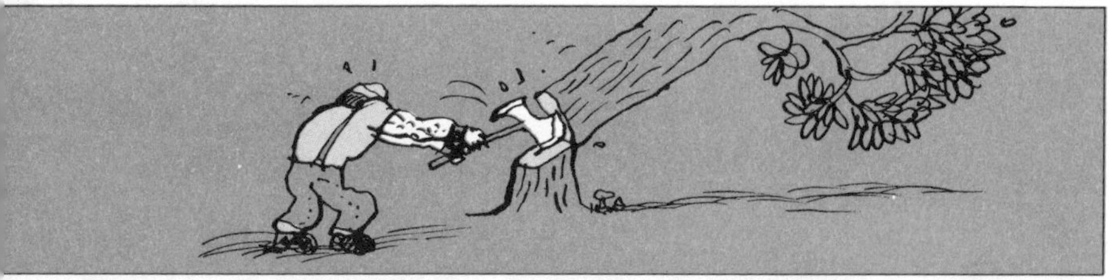

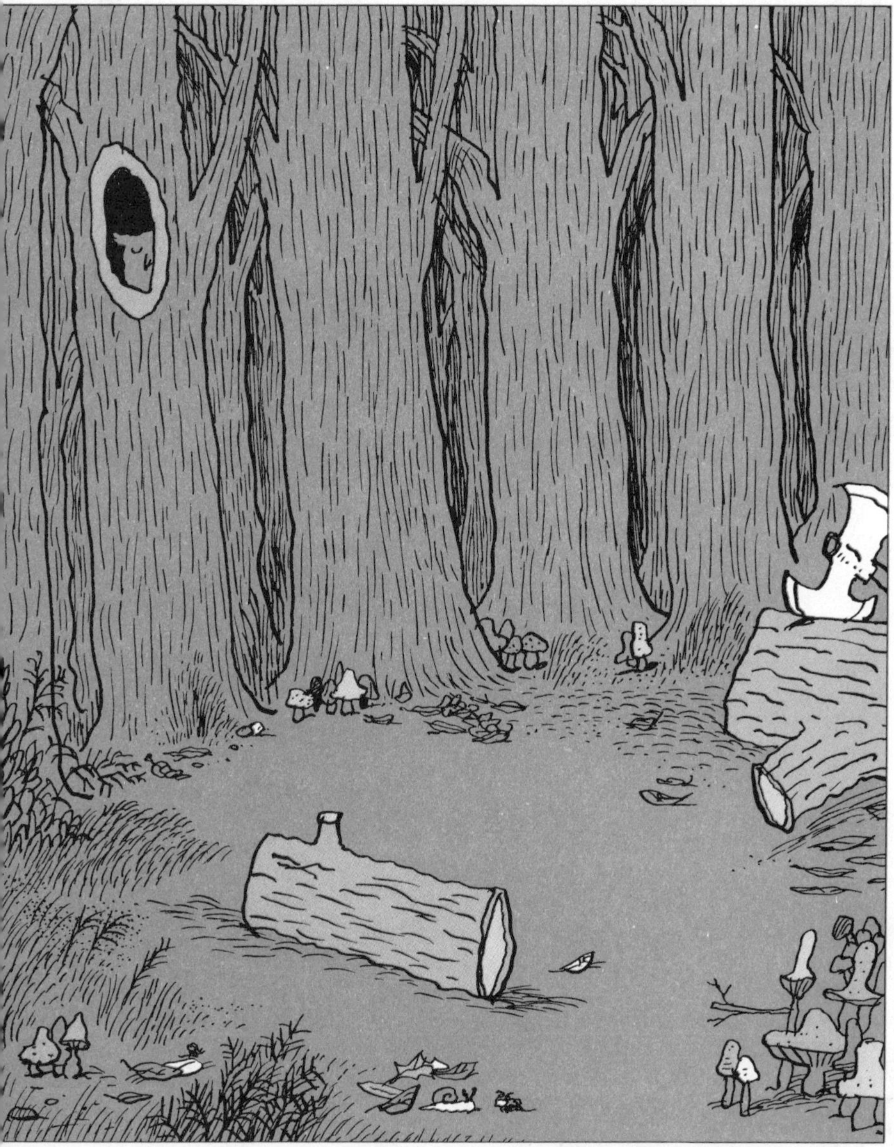

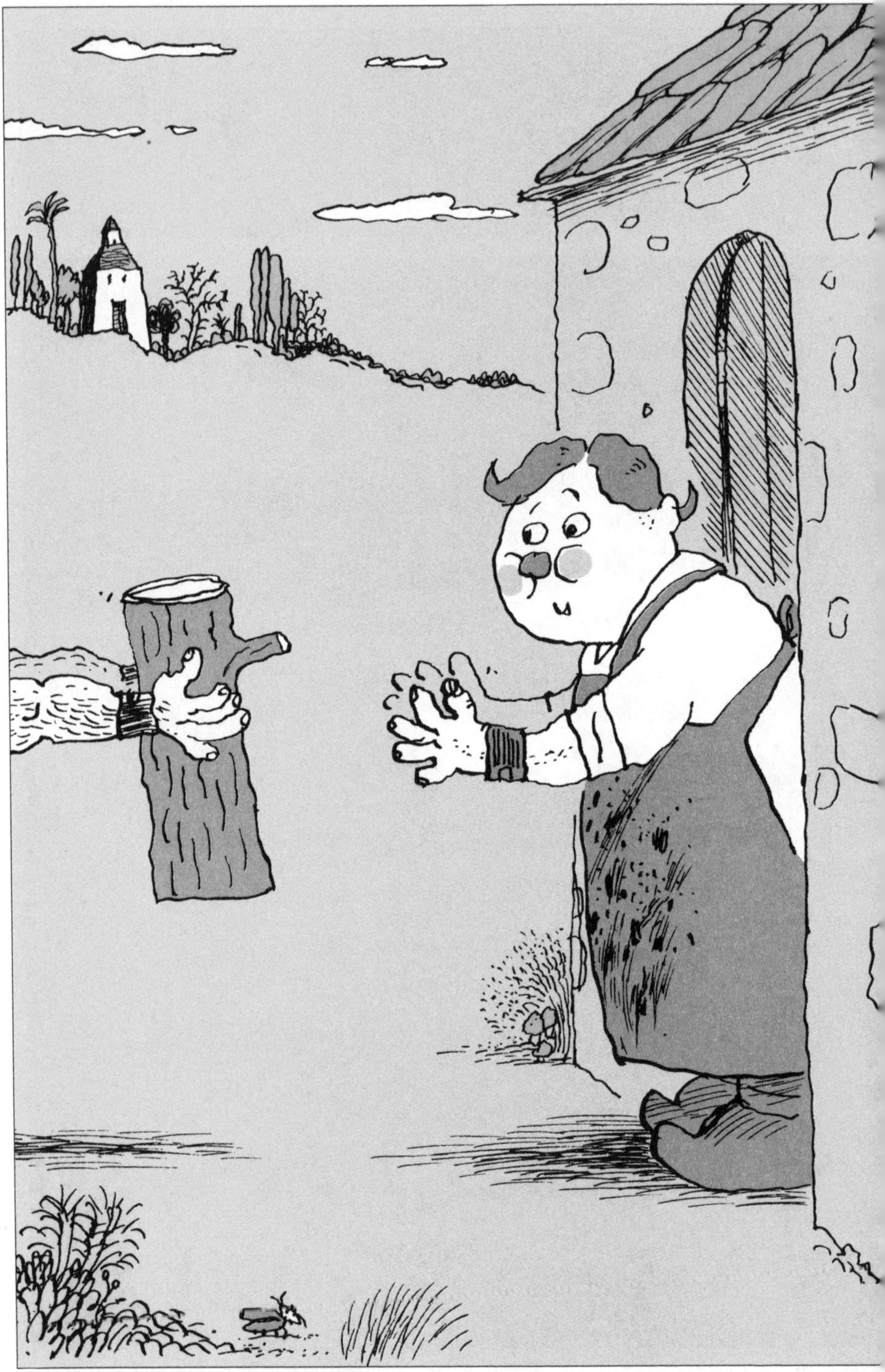

CHAPTER ONE

MR. CHERRY

ONCE there was a piece of wood.

When Mr. Cherry the carpenter saw it, he said, "This will make a fine table leg."

As he raised his hatchet to chop the bark off, a little voice said,

"Don't hurt me!"

1

"Who said that?" cried Mr. Cherry.

He looked around. No one was there.

Again he raised his hatchet—**WHACK!**

"Ouch!" cried the little voice.

"Stop that!" shouted Mr. Cherry, and he threw the wood against the wall.

BAM!

Mr. Cherry listened. He didn't hear the voice, so he picked up the wood and began scraping off the rough spots.

"That tickles!" laughed the little voice, and Mr. Cherry fainted—**THUD!**

CHAPTER TWO

GEPPETTO

KNOCK-KNOCK!

"Who's there?" called Mr. Cherry.

"Geppetto!" cried a poor wood carver, and in he came. "I want to make a puppet," he said. "A singing, dancing puppet to help me earn my bread. Will you give me wood for my puppet?"

"Gladly!" Mr. Cherry held out the talking piece of wood. All at once, the wood began to shake. It flew out of Mr. Cherry's hand and struck Geppetto's leg.

"Ow!" yelled Geppetto. "Why did you throw that wood at me?"

"I didn't," cried Mr. Cherry.

"You did!" cried Geppetto.

The two had a terrible fight, but it ended with a handshake.

Geppetto took the
piece of wood and limped
home to his cottage.

CHAPTER THREE

PINOCCHIO

"I AM your daddy," Geppetto said as he carved a head and eyes onto the piece of wood.

"And you are my Pinocchio."

Geppetto carved a nose.

It began to grow!

He carved a mouth. The puppet stuck out his tongue.

He carved arms and hands. The puppet pulled Geppetto's hair.

He carved legs and feet. The puppet kicked him.

"Bad boy!" cried Geppetto. But he showed his wooden son how to walk by putting one foot in front of the other. No sooner could Pinocchio walk than he began to run. He ran out the door and down the street.

Geppetto ran after him, but the puppet
ran faster.

People laughed to see the chase.

"Catch him!" Geppetto called to a pair of
police officers.

An officer grabbed Pinocchio by the nose.

"The puppet's only having fun,"
said a man.

"Geppetto has a temper," said a woman.
"He will break that puppet to bits!"

"Is that right?" said the officer.
He set Pinocchio down. The puppet took
off running.

And Geppetto? The officers took him
to jail.

CHAPTER FOUR

CRICKET

PINOCCHIO ran home. He found a big cricket on the wall.

"I'm Cricket," the cricket said. "A boy who runs away from his father will come to no good."

"Who cares?" said Pinocchio. "I'm leaving tomorrow so I won't have to go to school."

"If you don't go to school," said Cricket, "you'll grow up to be a donkey."

"Watch it, Cricket," warned Pinocchio.

"Why not get a job?" said Cricket.

"I don't want to work!" cried Pinocchio. "I want to play!"

"You're a blockhead," said Cricket.

Pinocchio grabbed a wooden hammer and threw it at Cricket.

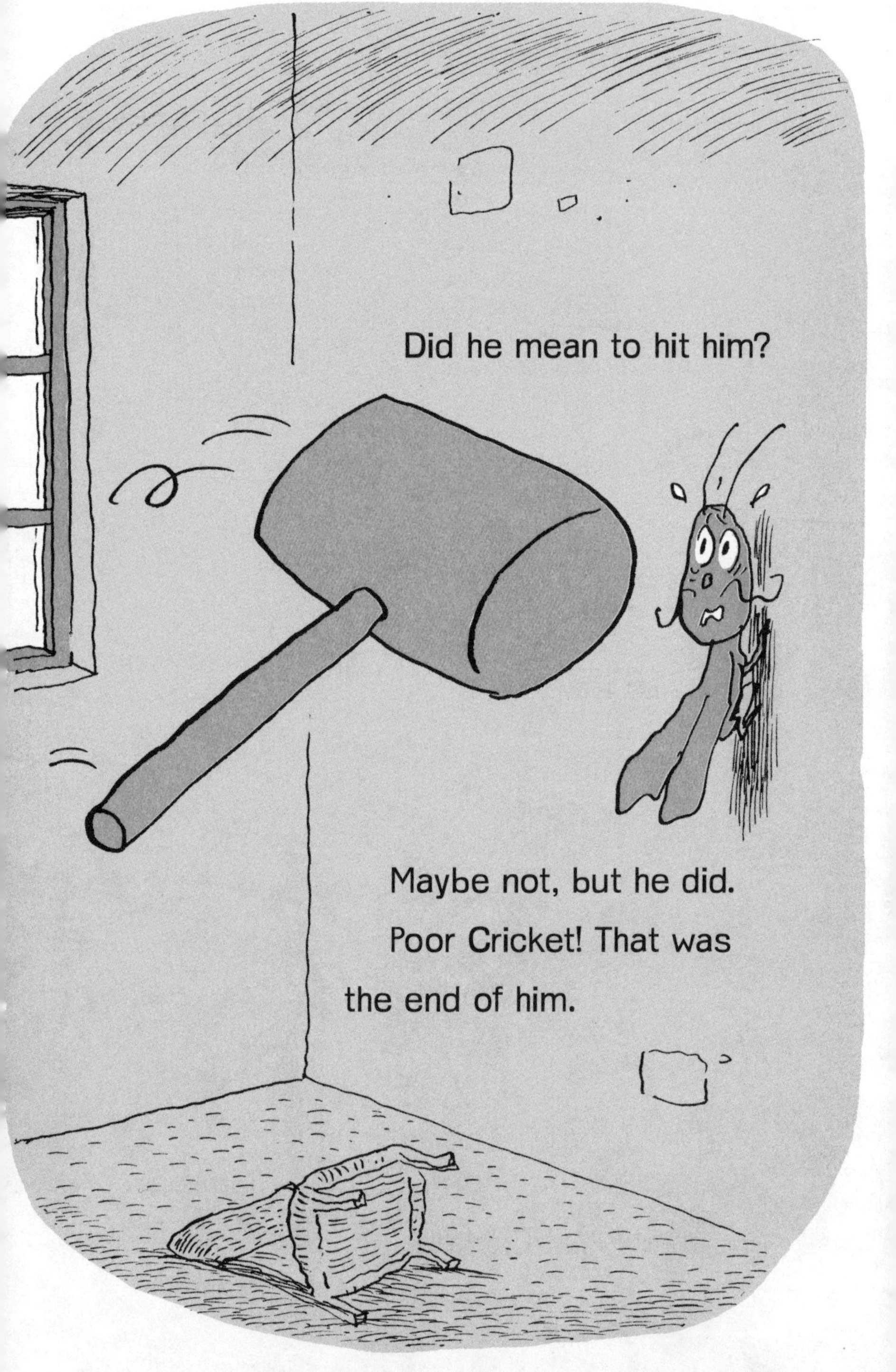

Did he mean to hit him?

Maybe not, but he did. Poor Cricket! That was the end of him.

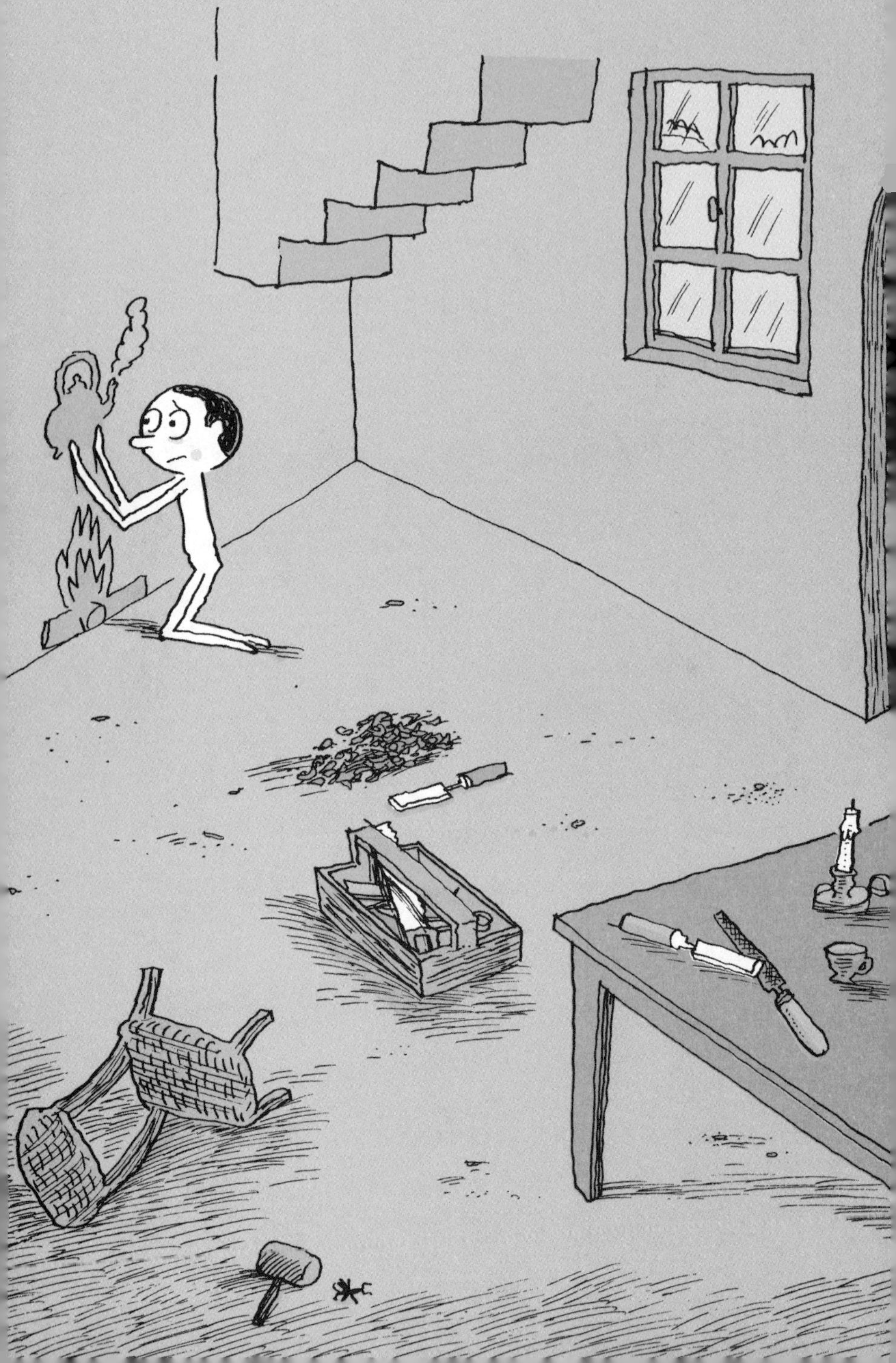

CHAPTER FIVE

HUNGRY!

PINOCCHIO was alone and hungry.
He ran to the fireplace, where a soup pot
was boiling. He tried to lift the lid, but he
discovered that the pot and fire were only
painted on the wall.

He searched the cottage for something
to eat. He found a little pan with hot coals.
But what was there to cook on the coals?
NOTHING!

Pinocchio sank to the floor. *Cricket was right*, he thought. *I shouldn't have run away. If Daddy were here, he'd feed me.*

Just then, Pinocchio spied an egg in a pile of wood shavings. He put a pot of water over the pan of coals and tapped the egg on the side.

CRRRRACK! Out popped a little chick.

"Thanks for breaking my shell," the chick called, and he flew out the window.

CHAPTER SIX

THE VILLAGE

A STORM blew in. Lightning flashed! Thunder crashed! Wind whipped the trees!

Pinocchio ran through the stormy night to the village to find something to eat. The shops were closed. Houses were dark. Dogs hurried back to their homes.

Pinocchio rang a doorbell. An old man in a nightcap looked down from a high window.

"Bread, please!" begged Pinocchio.

"Stay there!" the man called. He disappeared from the window. When he returned, he said, "Hold out your hands."

Pinocchio held out his hands for bread, but the man threw a bucket of water on him.

Pinocchio dragged himself home.

Cricket was right, he thought as he warmed his wet feet by the pan of coals. He fell asleep, and as he slept, his feet burned to ashes.

KNOCK-KNOCK!

Pinocchio woke up. "Who's there?"

"Your daddy!" cried Geppetto.

CHAPTER SEVEN

PEARS

PINOCCHIO jumped up, but he clattered to the floor.

"Open the door!" shouted Geppetto.

"I can't get to the door!" cried Pinocchio. "I have no feet!"

"Fibber!" roared Geppetto. He climbed in through the window, hopping mad! But when he saw his puppet son lying on the floor, he took him up in his arms.

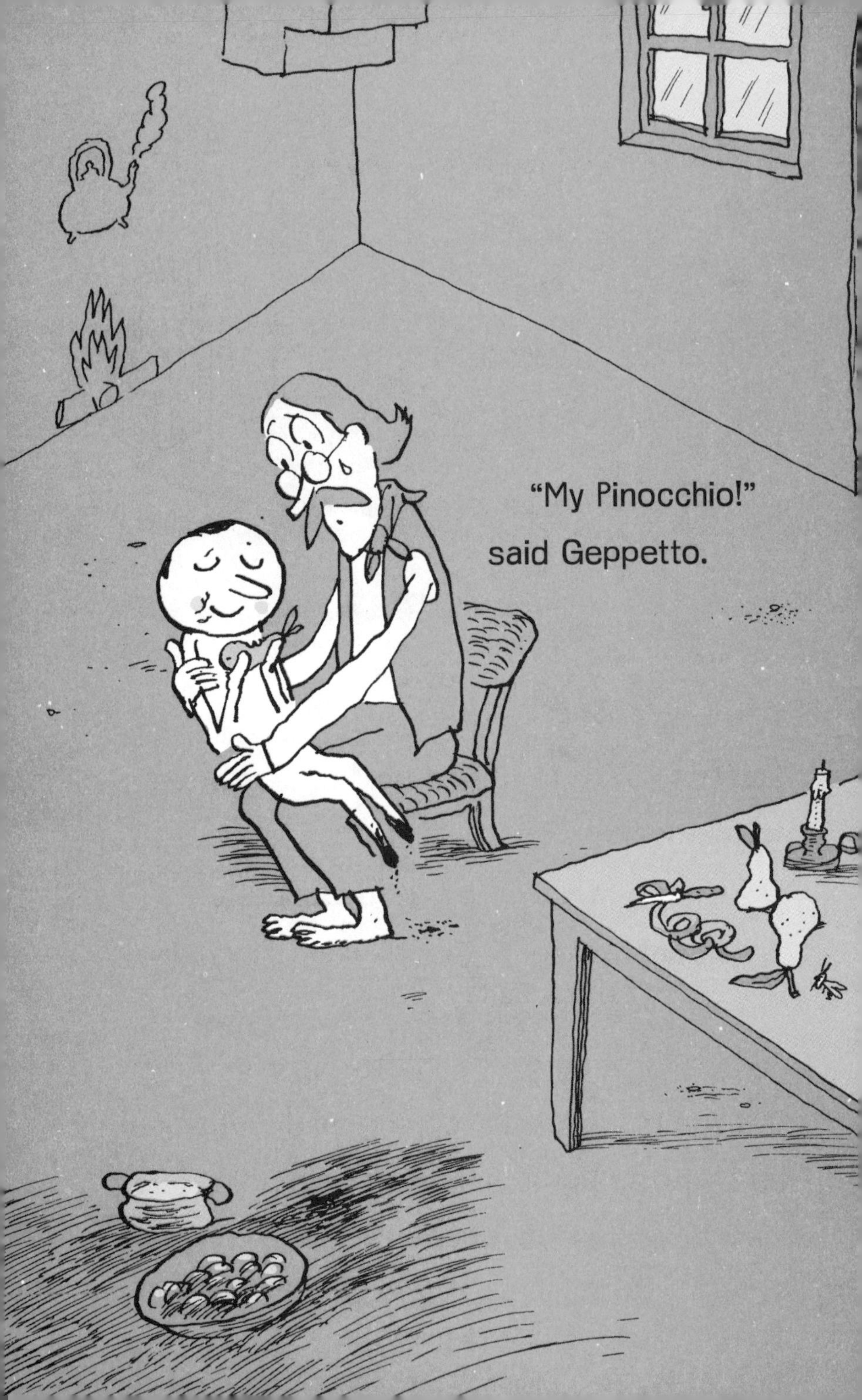

"My Pinocchio!"
said Geppetto.

Pinocchio told his daddy about the cricket, the chick, the storm, the bucket of water, and the hot coals. "And I'm still hungry," he cried.

Geppetto took three pears from his pocket. They were to have been his breakfast, but now he gave them to Pinocchio.

"Peel them for me!" cried the puppet.

"Eat every bit," said Geppetto, "for we never know what the world has in store for us."

But Pinocchio refused, so Geppetto peeled the pears for his son. Pinocchio gobbled them up, leaving the cores. He was still hungry, so he ate the peels. Then he ate the cores. At last his belly was full.

CHAPTER EIGHT

SPELLING BOOK

"MAKE ME new feet, Daddy," said Pinocchio.

"So you can run away again?" asked Geppetto.

"So I can go to school," said Pinocchio.

Geppetto's heart filled with love for his wooden son. He carved two new feet and fastened them to Pinocchio's legs.

Pinocchio skipped around the cottage. "What will I wear to school?"

Geppetto had no money, so he made Pinocchio tree-bark shoes, a paper jacket, and a bread-dough cap.

Pinocchio twirled with happiness in his new clothes. "Now I need a spelling book," he said.

"You shall have one!" Geppetto put on his
old warm coat and went out into the snow.

He came back with a spelling book.

"Where's your coat?" asked Pinocchio.

"It was too warm, so I sold it," said
Geppetto.

Pinocchio understood what his father had
done. He threw his arms around his neck
and kissed him.

CHAPTER NINE

MUSIC

IT STOPPED snowing, and Pinocchio set off for school. As he went, he heard flutes and drums. The music came from a little village by the sea.

"I'll go to school tomorrow," said Pinocchio, and off he ran to the village, where he found people waiting to get into a theater.

"What does that sign on the theater say?" Pinocchio asked a boy.

"It says PUPPET SHOW, TWENTY-FIVE CENTS," said the boy.

"Lend me the money," said Pinocchio.

"No," said the boy.

"I'll sell you my jacket for twenty-five cents," said Pinocchio.

"No!" said the boy.

"My spelling book?" asked Pinocchio, but the boy ran off.

"I'll buy the book," said a junkman, handing him twenty-five cents.

Pinocchio gave the book to him. Then he ran and bought a ticket, never thinking of Geppetto back home, shivering in the cold.

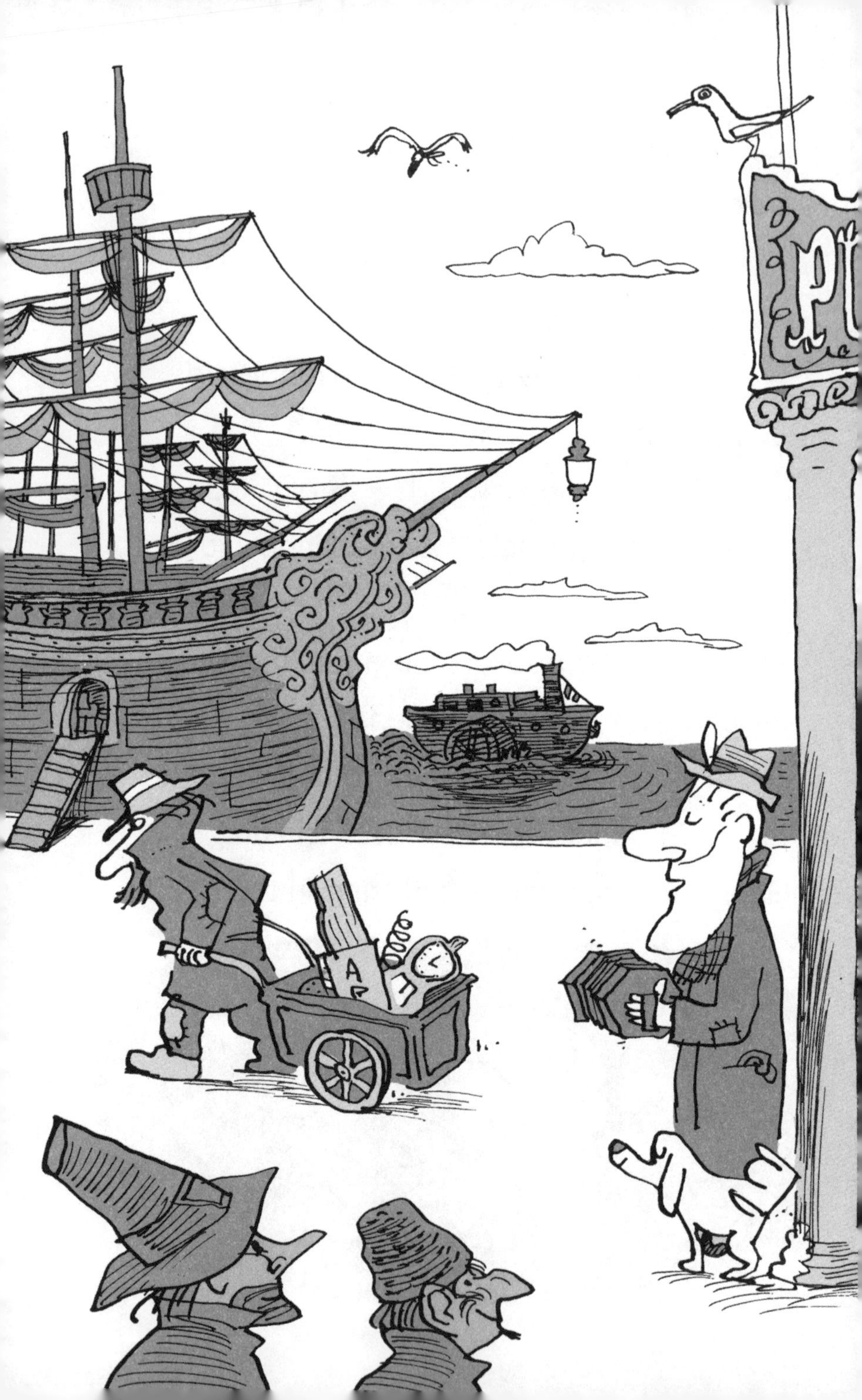

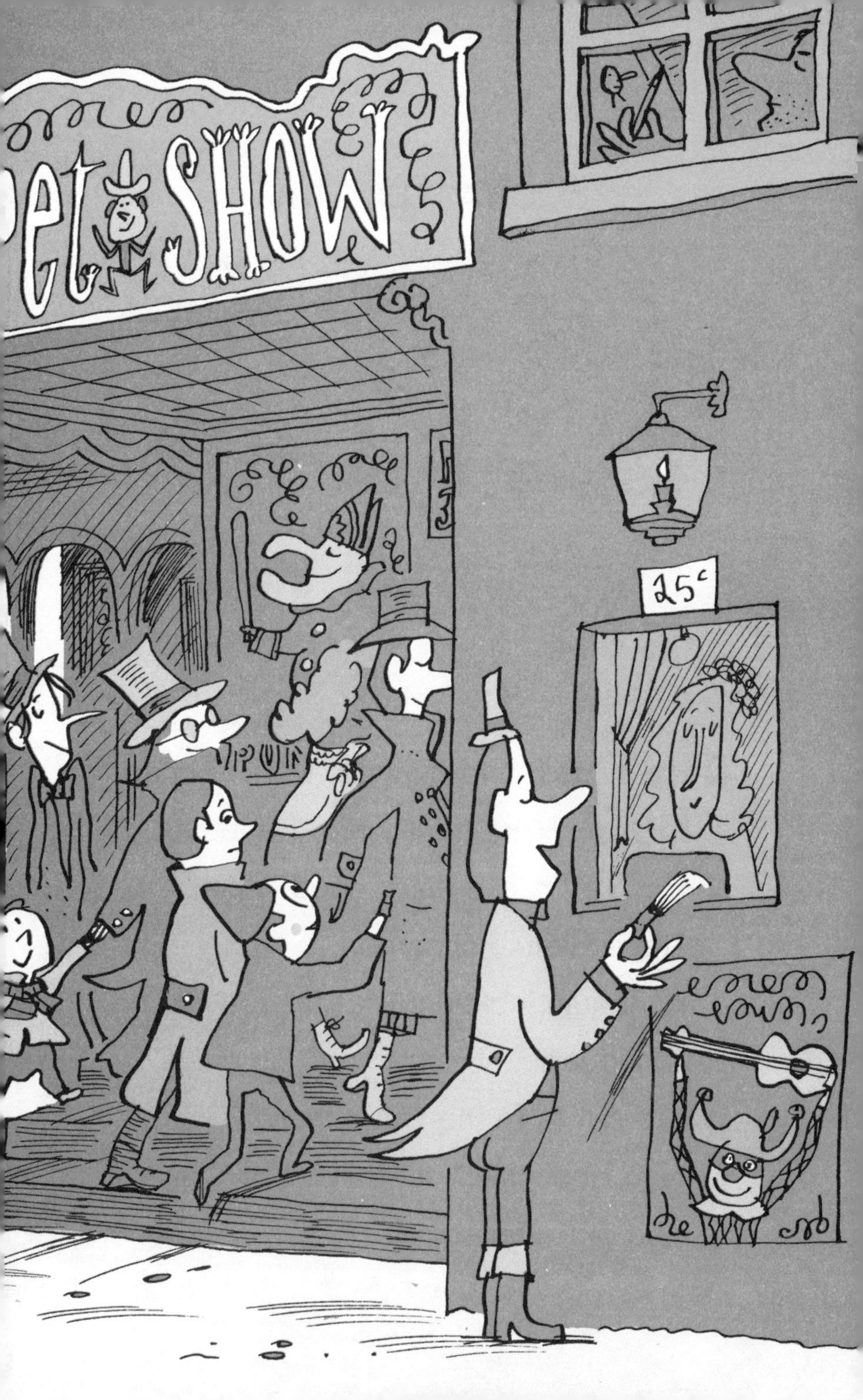
et SHOW
25¢

CHAPTER TEN

PUPPETS

ONSTAGE two puppets were fighting.

BOP! "Take that!" cried Harlequin.

POW! "Take that!" cried Punch.

The audience cheered.

Harlequin looked out at the crowd and saw Pinocchio. "I know you!" he cried. "We're cut from the same tree."

"I'm Pinocchio!" cried Pinocchio, and he leaped onto the stage.

The other puppets hugged him.

The audience shouted, "On with the show!"

But the puppets kept hugging and shouting, "Pinocchio! Pinocchio!"

THUMP, THUMP!

Fire-Eater, the Puppet Master, stomped onto the stage.

He was a giant man with a coal-black beard. "Finish the play!" he shouted. He grabbed Pinocchio by the nose and carried him away.

When the play ended, Harlequin found Fire-Eater in his kitchen, roasting a ram for his supper. Pinocchio was hanging from a nail on the wall.

"I'm out of wood!" boomed Fire-Eater. "Hand me that puppet. I'll toss him on the fire to roast my ram."

Harlequin didn't move.

"NOW!" roared Fire-Eater.

Harlequin slowly took
Pinocchio down from the nail.

CHAPTER ELEVEN

FIRE-EATER

"HELP, DADDY!" cried Pinocchio. "I
don't want to die."

Hearing Pinocchio's cries, Fire-Eater
sneezed. **"AH-CHOO!"**

"That's a good sign," Harlequin whispered.
"Fire-Eater only sneezes when he feels sorry
for someone."

Fire-Eater sneezed again. **"AH-CHOO!"**
Then he turned and called, "Guards!"

Two tall wooden guards appeared.

"Tie up Harlequin," ordered Fire-Eater. "Throw him onto the fire."

"No!" cried Pinocchio.

Harlequin dropped to the floor in fright.

"If they don't throw him onto the fire, how will I roast my ram?" roared Fire-Eater.

"Guards!" cried Pinocchio. "Toss me into the flames! I don't want Harlequin to die in my place."

"**AH-CHOO!**" sneezed Fire-Eater. "**AH-CHOO!** Oh, poor Harlequin. You're a good boy, Pinocchio. Tonight I'll eat my ram half-cooked."

All the puppets cheered and ran onto the stage, where they danced till dawn.

CHAPTER TWELVE

FOX & CAT

PINOCCHIO told Fire-Eater how
Geppetto had sold his coat to buy him a
spelling book.

"**AH-CHOO!**" sneezed Fire-Eater. "Oh,
poor Geppetto. Here, take these five gold
coins to him. "**AH-CHOO!**"

Pinocchio pocketed the coins and set
off for home.

He hadn't gone far when a fox with a
bad leg and a blind cat began walking
beside him.

"Greetings, Pinocchio," said Fox.

"You know my name?" asked the puppet.

"We know your father," said Cat.

"We saw him yesterday," added Fox,
"shivering from the cold."

"He won't shiver long," said Pinocchio,
"for I shall buy him a warm coat with
these." He showed them the gold coins.

Fox stared, and stopped limping for a
few steps. Cat, blind as he was, gazed at
the coins.

"Come with us to the Field of Miracles," said Fox.

"No, I must go home," said Pinocchio.

"Too bad," said Cat. "For if you bury coins in the Field of Miracles, a tree will grow."

"A tree with thousands of gold coins for leaves," added Fox.

"Thousands?" cried Pinocchio. "Let's go!"

CHAPTER THIRTEEN

THE GHOST

THE THREE walked until sunset, then stopped at an inn for supper. Fox and Cat feasted on chickens, rabbits, and fish, but Pinocchio was too excited to eat.

After dinner, they took a room.

"Wake us at midnight," Fox told the innkeeper.

The innkeeper winked. "Of course!"

Pinocchio fell asleep, dreaming of gold coins.

KNOCK-KNOCK!

"Wake up, Pinocchio!" said the innkeeper. "Your friends have gone. You are to meet them at the Field of Miracles. But first, pay the bill!"

Pinocchio had to give the innkeeper one gold coin, then he set off into the dark night. He hadn't gone far when he saw a small glow on a tree trunk.

"*I am Cricket's ghost,*" said the glow. "*Go home to your father!*"

"I will," said Pinocchio. "After I get him thousands of gold coins."

"*Never trust those who promise quick riches,*" warned the ghost. "*Go home!*"

"No!" cried Pinocchio.

"*Then heaven protect you from murderers*," said the ghost, and the glow faded.

CHAPTER FOURTEEN

MURDERERS!

"I DON'T believe in murderers," said Pinocchio to himself as he walked on down the road.

Footsteps sounded. Pinocchio turned and saw two hooded figures running toward him. One was tall, one was short.

"Murderers!" he squeaked.

As they grabbed him, Pinocchio popped the gold coins into his mouth.

"Give us your money!" growled the tall murderer.

Pinocchio shook his head no.

"Then we'll kill you," said the short one. "And your daddy, too."

"Nut ma diddy!" said Pinocchio with his jaws shut tight.

"Spit out the coins!" cried the tall one.

Pinocchio shook his head again.

The short murderer tried to pry Pinocchio's mouth open.

Pinocchio poked the coins into his cheek with his tongue and . . .

CHOMP!

Pinocchio bit off the short murderer's hand! It fell to the ground, and he saw that it wasn't a hand at all but a cat's paw.

Pinocchio twisted away and took off running.

The murderers chased after him.

Pinocchio climbed a tall pine tree.

The murderers set it on fire.

Pinocchio leaped to the ground and ran.

He jumped over a ditch filled with water.

The murderers leaped, too, but . . .

SPLASH!

Pinocchio had escaped. He ran a little farther and looked over his shoulder. The murderers were still after him!

CHAPTER FIFTEEN

LITTLE HOUSE

FAR AWAY, Pinocchio spied a little white house. He ran faster. At last he reached the house and pounded on the door.

A blue-haired girl came to a window.

"Opie da door!" Pinocchio cried as best he could with four gold coins in his mouth.

Right then, the tall murderer grabbed him. "Open your mouth!" he ordered.

Pinocchio kept his mouth shut.

"Then die!" said the short murderer.

The two pulled out knives and stabbed Pinocchio. But the puppet was made of good hard wood, and the knives broke.

"Let's hang him!" cried the tall one.

The murderers tied a rope around his neck and hanged the puppet from an oak tree. Then they sat down to wait for him to stop kicking.

They waited for hours, but Pinocchio kept kicking.

"He'll be dead by tomorrow," said the tall one. "Let's come back."

They left Pinocchio all alone.

"Daddy . . ." Pinocchio said. His eyes closed and he stopped kicking.

CHAPTER SIXTEEN

THE FAIRY

THE GIRL with blue hair was a fairy. From her window, she saw the puppet dangling from the tree.

She clapped three times. A giant falcon flew to her.

"Falcon," said Blue Fairy, "snip the rope
that holds the puppet on the oak tree, and
lay him on the grass."
Falcon flew off.

Blue Fairy clapped twice. A giant poodle
pulled up in a carriage drawn by mice.

"Lancelot," said Blue Fairy, "bring me
the puppet lying on the grass beneath
the oak tree."

When Lancelot returned, Blue Fairy carried Pinocchio to a small room and put him to bed. She called three doctors.

"Dr. Crow, is the puppet alive or dead?" she asked.

"He's dead," said Dr. Crow. "Unless he's alive."

"He's alive," said Dr. Owl. "Unless he's dead."

"I know this puppet, Pinocchio," said
Dr. Cricket. "He broke his father's heart."

A snuffling sound filled the room.
Pinocchio was crying!

CHAPTER SEVENTEEN

RABBITS

"YOU HAVE a fever, Pinocchio," Blue
Fairy said, stirring white powder into a glass
of water. "Drink this."

"Is it bitter?" asked Pinocchio.

Blue Fairy nodded.

"I'd rather die than drink it!" cried
Pinocchio.

The door flew open. In came four black
rabbits carrying a small coffin.

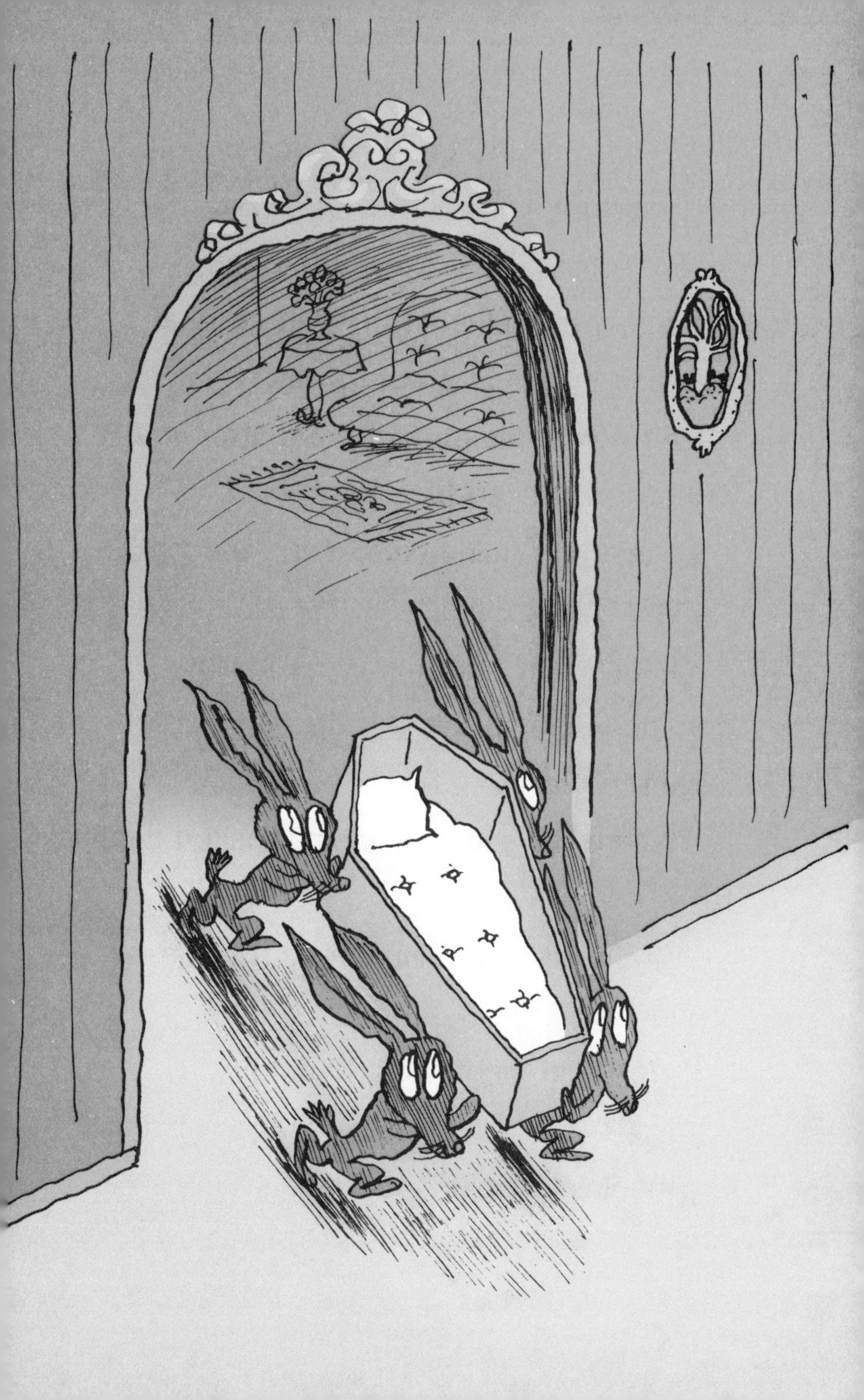

"I'm not dead!" cried Pinocchio.

"You soon will be," said a rabbit.

Pinocchio gulped down the bitter medicine. In an instant, he felt good as new and the rabbits went away.

"Why were those murderers after you, Pinocchio?" asked Blue Fairy.

"I had four gold coins," said Pinocchio. "But . . . I lost them."

He had really put the coins in his pocket. When he told this lie, his nose began to grow.

"Where did you lose them?" asked Blue Fairy.

"In the woods." Pinocchio's nose grew longer still.

"We'll find them," said Blue Fairy.

"No, I swallowed the coins when I drank my medicine," said Pinocchio.

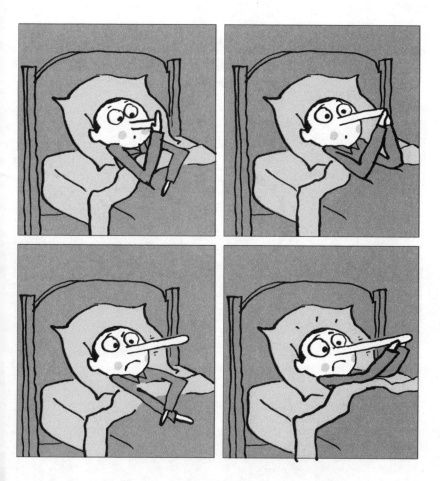

His nose grew until it hit the wall.

Blue Fairy laughed. "Some lies have short legs. Others have long noses," she said. "Your lies are the long-nosed sort."

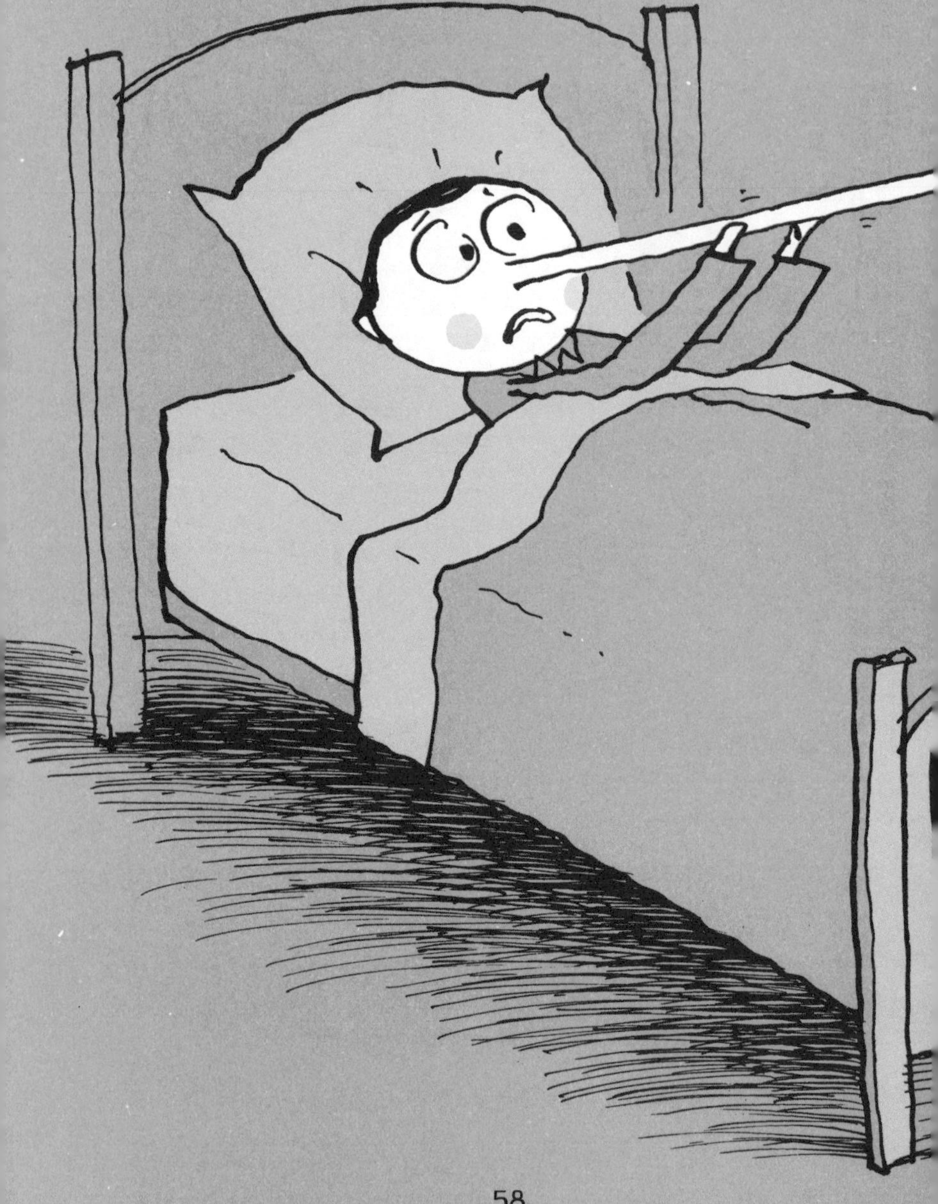

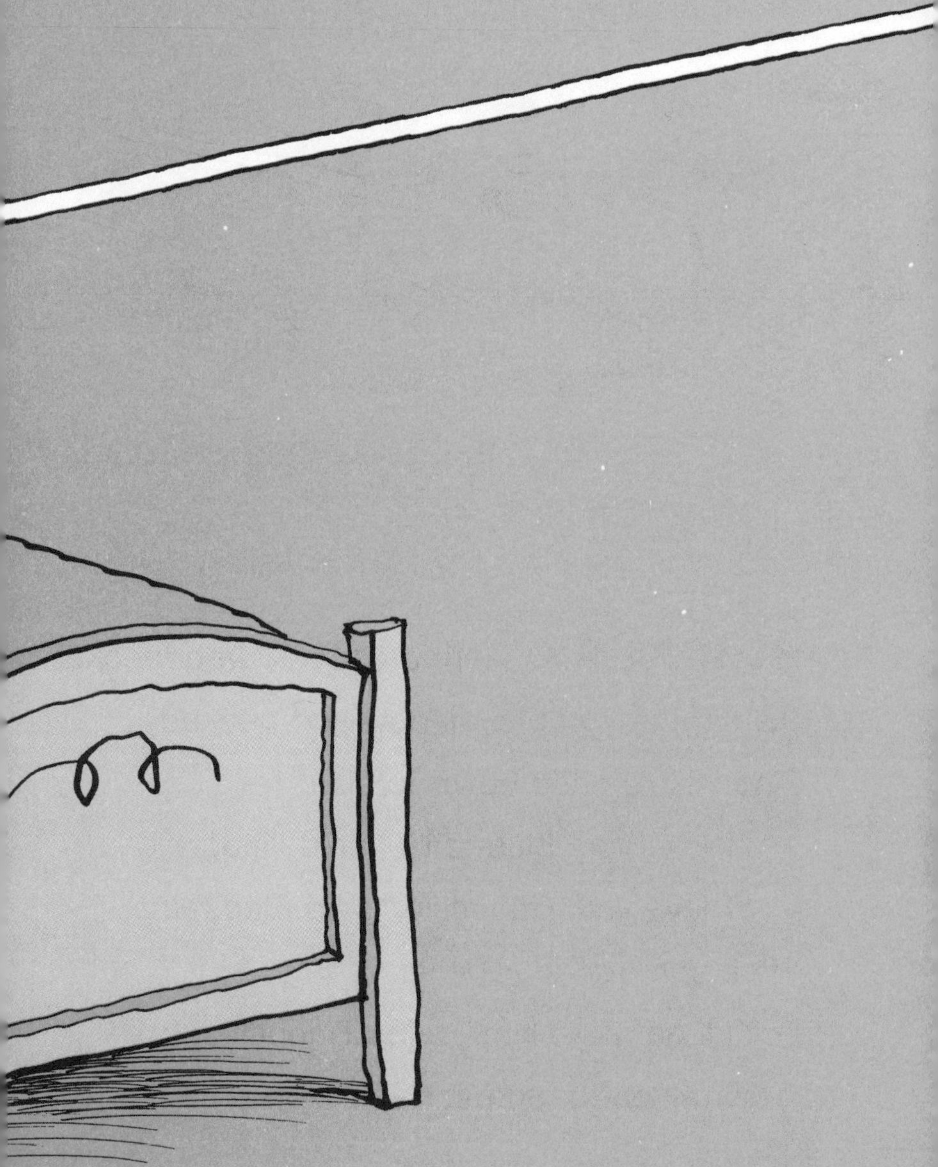

CHAPTER EIGHTEEN

GOLD COINS

BLUE FAIRY clapped once. A woodpecker flew in through the window and pecked Pinocchio's nose down to size.

"I love you, Blue Fairy," said Pinocchio.

"I love you, Pinocchio," said Blue Fairy. "I've sent for your father."

"I'll go meet him!" cried Pinocchio.

"Stay on the forest path," warned Blue Fairy.

Pinocchio hurried off. As he passed the oak tree, out stepped Fox and Cat. Cat's front paw was missing.

"Where were you?" asked Fox.

Pinocchio told them about the murderers.

"Did they get your gold coins?" asked Cat.

"No." Pinocchio pulled them from his pocket. "See?"

"Yessss," the blind cat hissed softly. "I mean, no."

"Let's go to the Field of Miracles now!" said Fox.

"It's not far," said Cat. "Just outside Chumptrap City."

Pinocchio thought of his daddy and Blue Fairy and Cricket, but he wanted that tree of coins! So he went with Fox and Cat to the field. There, he dug a hole and buried his coins.

"Now go for a walk in Chumptrap City," said Cat. "When you come back, you'll find your tree."

"Good-bye, Pinocchio!" said Fox and Cat as he went off.

CHAPTER NINETEEN

THE PARROT

PINOCCHIO walked through Chumptrap. Then he raced back to the field.

Where was his tree?

"*Ha ha!*" called a parrot from a nearby branch. "*Fox and Cat stole your coins.*"

Pinocchio dropped to his knees and dug in the dirt. His coins were gone.

"*Gone!*" screeched the parrot. "*Gone!*"

Pinocchio ran to the Chumptrap Courthouse.

"Judge, I've been robbed!" he cried.

The judge banged his gavel, and two big, furry guards ran into the courtroom.

"Someone stole his gold," said the judge. "Take him to jail!"

"Not me!" cried Pinocchio, but the guards led him off to a cell.

The cell door slammed. There Pinocchio
stayed for four long months, until the emperor
declared that everyone in Chumptrap City
should come to a celebration, and the jailhouse
doors were thrown wide open.

CHAPTER TWENTY

SNAKE!

FREED from jail, Pinocchio ran down a muddy road toward Blue Fairy's house. He hoped his daddy was there waiting for him. All of a sudden, he came to a huge snake blocking the road.

"Mr. Snake, let me go by," said Pinocchio.

The snake only closed its eyes.

"I'm going to see my daddy," Pinocchio said. "Get out of my way!"

The snake didn't move.

Pinocchio raised a foot to step over it, but the snake reared up. Flames shot from its eyes! Smoke billowed from its tail!

HISS!

Pinocchio jumped back, flipped over, and landed upside down with his head in the mud.

Seeing Pinocchio's feet kicking the air, the snake laughed so hard, he laughed himself to death.

Pinocchio pulled his head out of the mud, leaped over the snake, and ran for Blue Fairy's little white house.

If only he hadn't been hungry! For when Pinocchio spied some grapes and ran into a field to pick some . . .

SNAP!

He got caught in a weasel trap.

CHAPTER TWENTY-ONE

THE WATCHDOG

DARK came on. Pinocchio saw a farmer walking toward him holding a lantern.

"So it's *you* stealing my chickens!" the farmer said.

"No! I was only picking grapes," said Pinocchio.

"If you'll steal grapes, you'll steal a chicken," said the farmer. He opened the trap, picked Pinocchio up, and carried him home.

When he reached his yard, he tossed
Pinocchio into a large pen with a doghouse
and a chicken coop inside.

"My watchdog died today," he said. "You
can take his place."

He fastened a spiked collar around
Pinocchio's neck and clipped on a chain.

"If any thieves show up, **BARK!**" said the
farmer. Then he went into his house, leaving
the puppet hungry, scared, and alone.

Pinocchio crept into the doghouse and
fell asleep.

CHAPTER TWENTY-TWO

WEASELS!

VOICES woke Pinocchio. He poked his head out of the doghouse and saw four weasels tunneling under the fence.

"Where's the regular watchdog?" asked a weasel.

"Dead," said Pinocchio.

"Too bad," said another weasel. "He always let us catch chickens if we gave him one."

"Is that right?" said Pinocchio.

The weasel nodded. "You look like a nice dog," he said. "We'll make the same deal with you."

The weasels jimmied the lock on the chicken coop door and slipped inside.

Pinocchio ran to the chicken coop, slammed the door, and barked,

WOOF! WOOF! WOOF!

The farmer jumped out of bed, grabbed a sack, and ran to the yard. He rushed into the chicken coop and came out with a sack full of weasels.

"Good job!" said the farmer. He unbuckled Pinocchio's collar. "You've paid for your grapes. Go on home now."

CHAPTER TWENTY-THREE

Here Lies Blue Fairy,
Her Heart Broken
by Pinocchio

THE PIGEON

PINOCCHIO ran straight to the little white house. But the house was gone. In its place stood a block of marble. The image of a beautiful girl who looked like Blue Fairy was carved into the stone. And words that said:

HERE LIES BLUE FAIRY,
HER HEART BROKEN BY PINOCCHIO

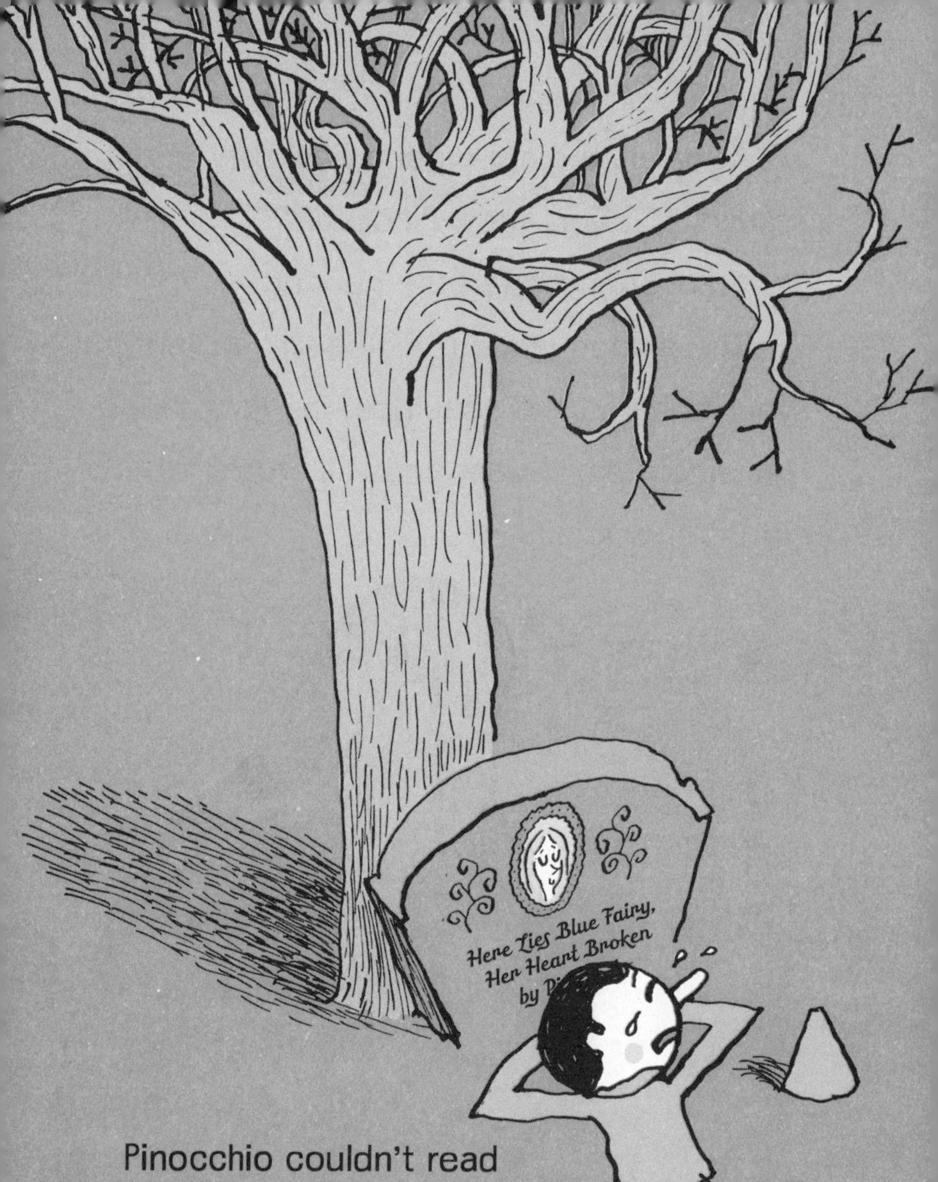
Here Lies Blue Fairy,
Her Heart Broken
by

Pinocchio couldn't read the words, but he knew what a tombstone was. He cried all night for Blue Fairy.

At dawn, a giant pigeon flew over and called, "Do you know Pinocchio?"

"That's me!" cried the puppet.

The pigeon landed beside him. "I left your father at the seashore," he said. "He's building a small boat and will cross the sea to look for you."

"I must go to him!" cried Pinocchio.

"Hop on my back," said the pigeon. He took to the air with his little passenger and flew all night. As the sun rose, he landed near the sea. Before Pinocchio could thank him, the pigeon flew off.

Fishermen lined the shore. They were pointing at a small boat far out to sea.

My daddy is in that boat! thought Pinocchio. He climbed to the top of a huge rock and waved his cap.

Geppetto saw him. He waved back!

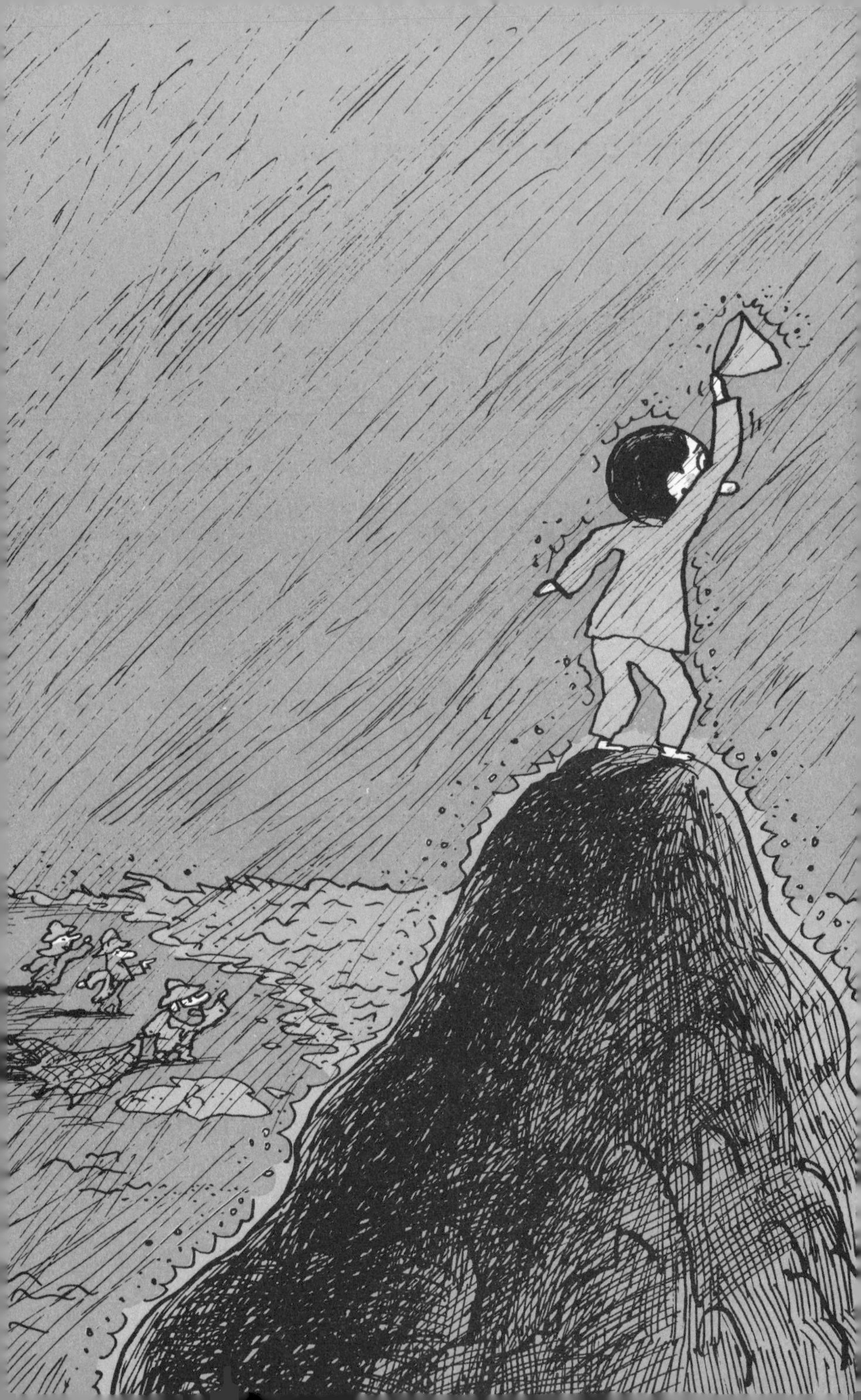

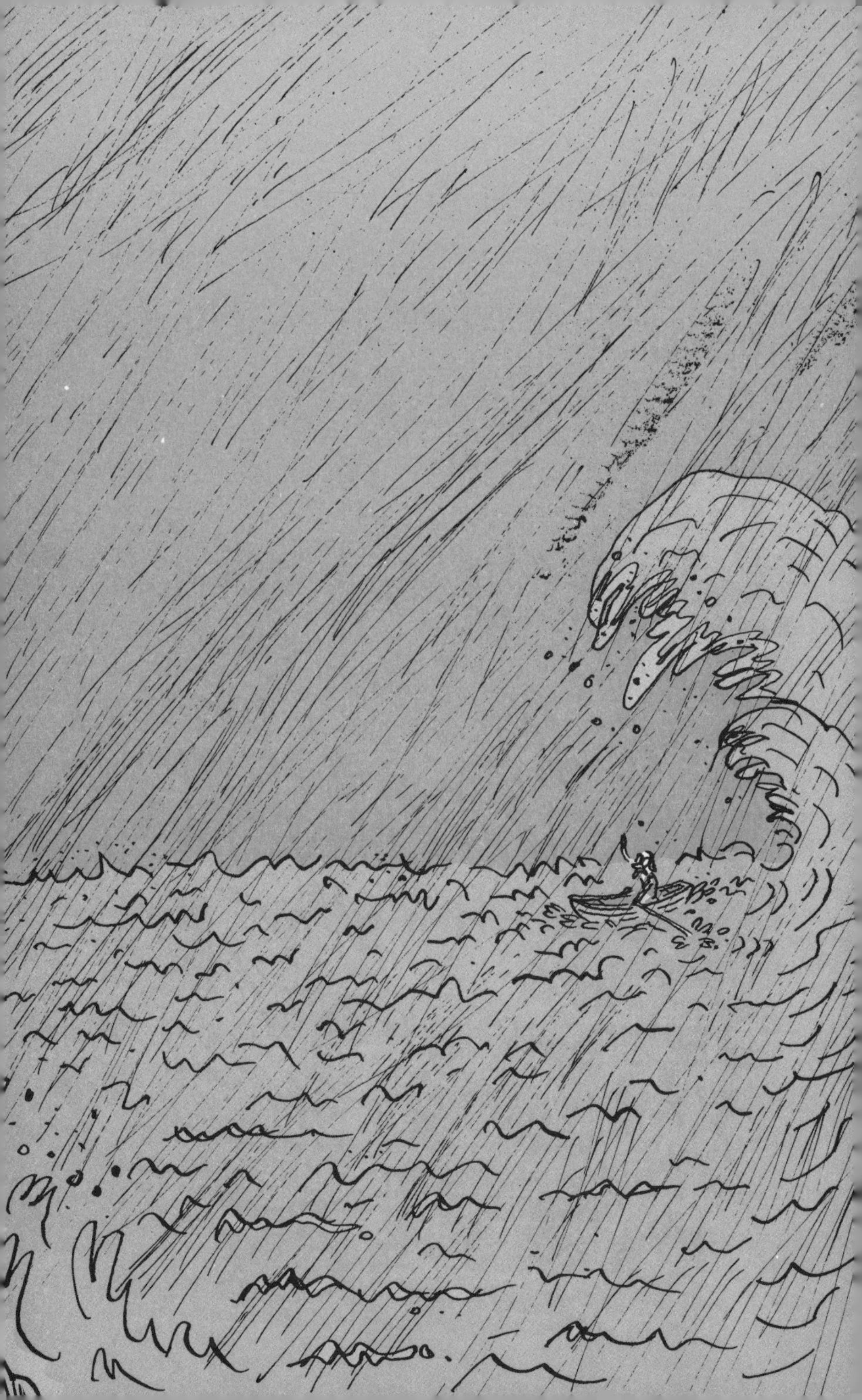

Just then, an enormous wave crashed onto the boat, flipping it over.

"I will save you, Daddy!" cried Pinocchio. He dove from the rock and swam out to sea.

CHAPTER TWENTY-FOUR

BUSY-BEE VILLAGE

PINOCCHIO swam until a wave tossed him onto an island.

A dolphin swam by. Pinocchio called, "Have you seen my daddy rowing a small boat?"

"The rowboat sank in the storm," said the dolphin. "Your daddy was swallowed by the giant shark."

"Poor Daddy!" cried Pinocchio. "It's all because he went looking for me!" With a heavy heart, he walked down a road until he came to Busy-Bee Village.

"Will you give me a nickel to buy food?" Pinocchio asked a man pulling a coal cart.

"I'll give you four nickels if you help me pull this cart," said the man.

"That's too hard!" said Pinocchio.

A man carrying bricks came by.

"Will you give me a nickel to buy food?" asked Pinocchio.

"I'll give you five nickels if you help me
carry these bricks," said the man.

"They're too heavy!" said Pinocchio.

A woman carrying two jugs of water
came along.

"May I have a drink, please?" asked
Pinocchio.

The woman handed him a jug. Pinocchio drank and drank.

"If you carry a jug for me, I'll give you something to eat," she added.

Pinocchio picked up the jug and walked with the woman to her house, where he ate a fine supper. When he finished, he looked up and saw that the woman's hair had turned blue!

CHAPTER TWENTY-FIVE

A BOY

"BLUE FAIRY!" cried Pinocchio. "I saw your tombstone!"

"But here I am, alive," said Blue Fairy.

"My daddy is dead," said Pinocchio. "He went searching for me and was eaten by a shark."

"My poor Pinocchio," said Blue Fairy. "I am here for you. Last time I saw you, I was a girl. Now I've changed into a woman."

"I want to change from a puppet to a boy," said Pinocchio.

"Boys study and go to school," said Blue Fairy.

"Oh," said Pinocchio.

"Boys tell the truth," said Blue Fairy.

"And I tell lies," said Pinocchio.

"You do," said Blue Fairy. "But you can stop, for you have a good heart."

"What else do I have to do to become a boy?" asked Pinocchio.

"Boys get jobs and work," Blue Fairy said.

"I don't want a job!" cried Pinocchio. "But I don't want to stay a puppet forever, either. I will do as you say, Blue Fairy."

Blue Fairy smiled. "You can do it, Pinocchio."

CHAPTER TWENTY-SIX

SCHOOL!

THE NEXT DAY, Pinocchio went to
school. A skinny boy named Lampwick
teased him for being a puppet. He tied
strings to Pinocchio's hands and feet
to make him dance.

"Don't!" warned Pinocchio.

Another boy, Eugene, yanked off his cap.
Pinocchio kicked him.

A boy named Federico grabbed his nose. Pinocchio elbowed him.

Pinocchio always stood up for himself. In time, the lads stopped picking on him, and he became well liked. Even the teacher praised him.

But the teacher warned him, "Watch out for these boys, Pinocchio. They are no-good rascals!"

On his way to school one morning, Pinocchio met his friends.

"A giant shark has been spotted offshore," cried Lampwick. "Come with us now to see it!"

"A giant shark?" said Pinocchio. Could it be the shark that had swallowed his daddy? he wondered. "I will go see this shark right after school."

"You think the shark will wait?" said Eugene.

"Come!" said Federico.

"We can be back in an hour."

"Let's go!" said Pinocchio,
and the boys took off running
to the sea.

CHAPTER TWENTY-SEVEN

FIGHT!

THE BOYS reached the seashore.
Pinocchio didn't see any shark.

His schoolmates began to laugh.

"We got you to skip school!" Lampwick
called.

"You're so good it makes us look bad!"
said Eugene.

"Now you look bad, too," said Federico.

How Pinocchio had hoped to see that giant shark!

"You rascals!" he shouted at the boys.

They came at him with their fists. There were seven of them and only one Pinocchio, but he held them off.

A boy grabbed Pinocchio's schoolbook and threw it at him. It missed, but it hit Eugene and he dropped to the sand. The other boys raced away.

Pinocchio wet his handkerchief with seawater and held it to Eugene's head.

A police officer came by. "What have you done to this boy?" he shouted.

"It wasn't me!" cried Pinocchio.

"Is this your book?" asked the officer.

"Yes," said Pinocchio truthfully.

"Come with me!" said the police officer.

He left Eugene in the care of some

fishermen and marched Pinocchio to town.
As they went, a gust of wind blew Pinocchio's
cap off.

"Go get it, quick!" said the police officer.

Pinocchio ran for his cap and then he kept
on running.

"Wingfoot!" cried the officer. "Get him!"

Pinocchio turned to see a fierce dog
chasing him!

CHAPTER TWENTY-EIGHT

WINGFOOT

PINOCCHIO ran from the dog and leaped into the ocean.

Wingfoot leaped in after him.

"I can't swim!" cried Wingfoot. "Help me, Pinocchio!"

"Will you stop chasing me?" asked Pinocchio.

"Yes," cried Wingfoot. "Hurry!"

Pinocchio grabbed Wingfoot's tail and pulled him to the beach. Then, to be safe, he jumped back into the sea.

"You saved me, Pinocchio!" called Wingfoot. "Maybe I'll save you one day."

Pinocchio swam away, keeping a lookout for that shark. As he swam by a cave on the shore, he felt something lifting him up. He was caught in a fishnet!

Out of the cave came a monstrous fisherman.

"Fish for supper!" he sang, hauling the net into his cave. He tossed the fish into a bucket: "Flounder, sea bass, goatfish." He tossed in Pinocchio. "Sea slug."

"I'm a puppet!" said Pinocchio.

"Puppet fish?" The fisherman licked his lips. "Sounds delicious!"

"I talk!" cried Pinocchio. "Doesn't that prove I'm not a fish?"

"Yum!" said the fisherman. He put his
skillet over the fire and poured in some oil.
When it was sizzling, he rolled Pinocchio in
flour until he was as white as
a statue. He grabbed him
by the neck and . . .

CHAPTER TWENTY-NINE

SAVED!

. . . WAS about to toss him into the skillet when a huge dog bounded into the cave. The dog snatched up Pinocchio in his mouth, ran from the cave, and set the puppet down in the road.

"Thank you, Wingfoot!" cried Pinocchio.

Wingfoot held out a paw. Pinocchio shook it, and the dog went on his way.

Pinocchio looked around. He was not far from Blue Fairy's house! He started down the road, and soon he met a kind-looking fisherman.

"Do you know what happened to Eugene, the boy who was hurt?" Pinocchio asked. "Is he dead?"

"Oh, no," said the fisherman. "He's gone home, very much alive."

Happy to hear it, Pinocchio walked on. It was dark by the time he reached Blue Fairy's house. How it had grown! Now it looked like a giant shell.

He knocked on the door. A snail appeared at the fourth-floor window.

"Be right there!" said Snail.

Pinocchio waited. "Hurry!" he called.

Snail appeared at the third-floor window. "Snails never hurry," he said.

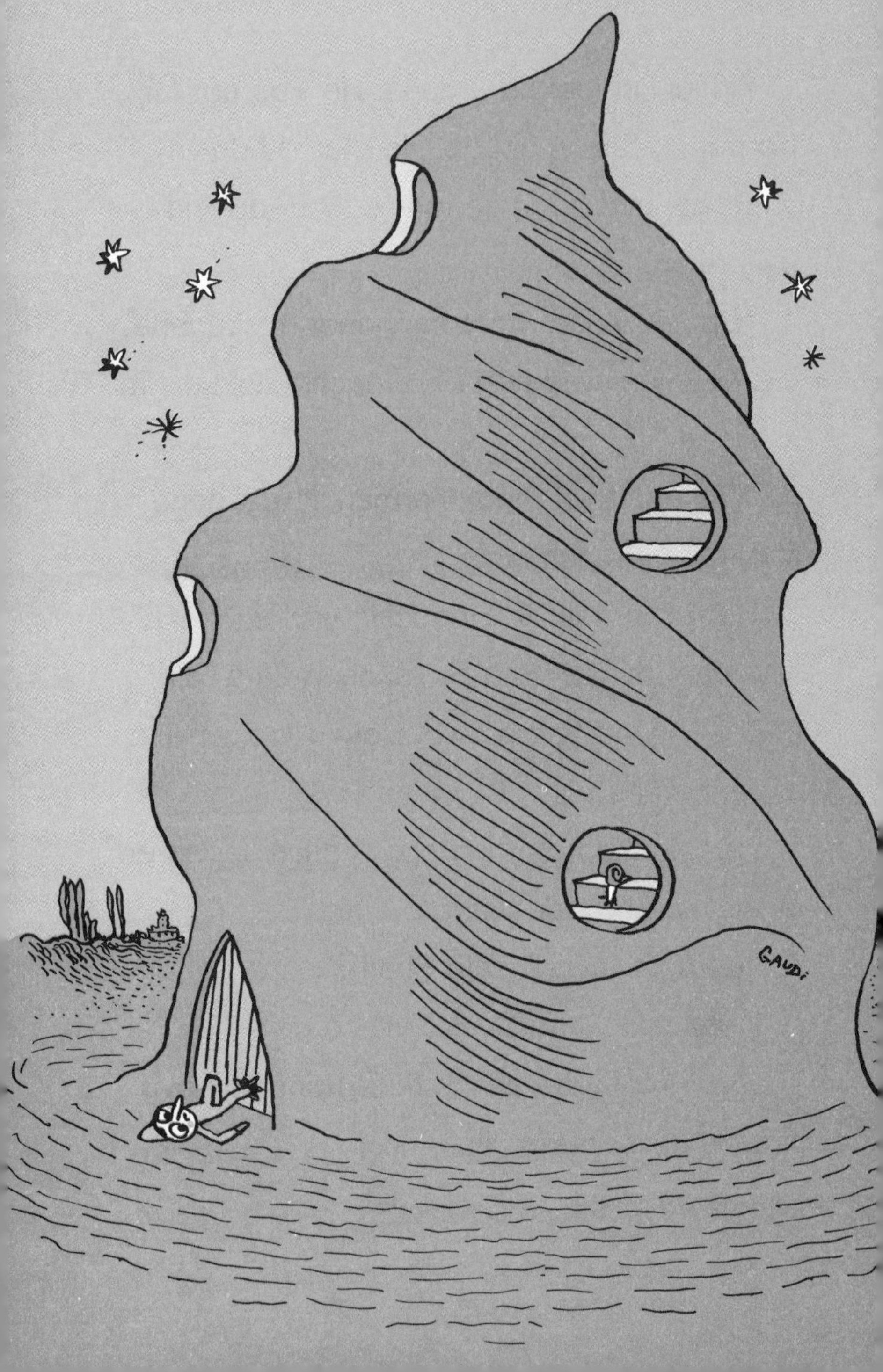
GAUDI

Pinocchio waited and waited. "Snail, hurry up!" he called.

Snail appeared at the second-floor window. "Snails never hurry," he said.

Pinocchio grew tired of waiting, and at last he gave the door a kick.

BAM! His foot went through the door. He couldn't pull it out, so Pinocchio spent the rest of the night sleeping with his foot stuck in the door.

When he woke, he was in bed. Blue Fairy was at his side.

"Do you forgive me?" Pinocchio asked.

"Yes," said Blue Fairy. "One last time."

Pinocchio went back to school. He behaved and made good grades.

And one night Blue Fairy said, "Tomorrow, Pinocchio, you will change from a puppet to a boy. We will have a party!"

"Thank you, Blue Fairy," said Pinocchio.
"If only my daddy were here to see me
become a boy."

CHAPTER THIRTY

LAMPWICK

THE NEXT DAY was Saturday. Pinocchio wanted to go ask his friends to the party.

"Come home before dark," said Blue Fairy.

Pinocchio ran from house to house, inviting all his friends. He went to Lampwick's house three times, but Lampwick wasn't there. Pinocchio was heading home when he spied him hiding under a porch.

"What are you doing under there?" asked the puppet.

"Waiting for a coach and driver to pick me up and take me to Toyland," said Lampwick.

"Don't go," said Pinocchio. "I'm having a party tonight!"

"Sorry," said Lampwick. "I'll be in Toyland, where there's no school and everyone plays all day. Come with me!"

"No," said Pinocchio. "I've promised Blue Fairy to be good."

But he stayed with Lampwick under that porch until dark, playing marbles and imagining Toyland.

"I must go home," said Pinocchio at last. "Good-bye, Lampwick."

"Wait!" cried Lampwick. "Here comes the coach."

CHAPTER THIRTY-ONE

TOYLAND

LITTLE MAN drove the coach, which was pulled by twelve small donkeys. It was filled with laughing, shouting children.

"Who's coming to Toyland?" Little Man called.

"I am!" cried Lampwick. There was no room inside the coach, so he sat with Little Man. "Come, Pinocchio!"

"Yes, come!" cried all the children.

Pinocchio sighed. He had promised Blue
Fairy he'd be good. And he wanted to make
his daddy proud. But all these laughing
children were going to Toyland. He wanted
to go, too! And so . . . he leaped onto the
back of a little donkey.

As they went, Pinocchio thought he
heard the donkey say, "You'll be sorry, as
I am, but by then it will be too late."

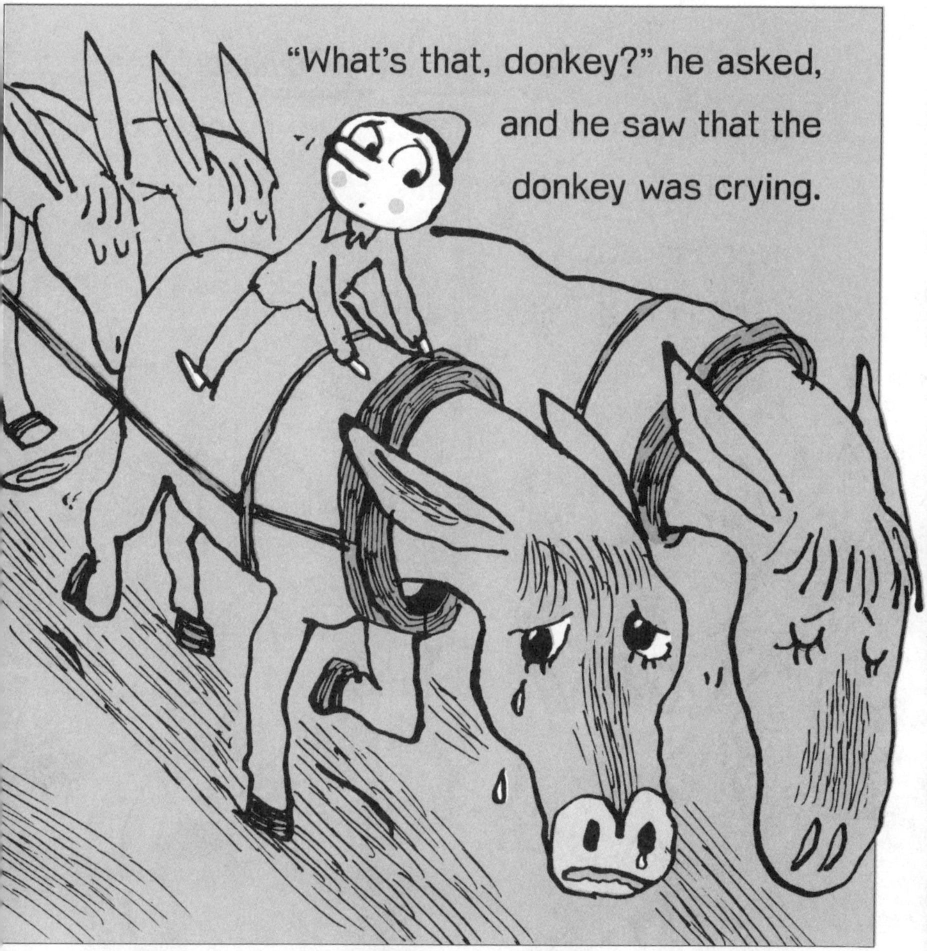
"What's that, donkey?" he asked,
and he saw that the
donkey was crying.

But when they reached Toyland, Pinocchio forgot all about the donkey. He joined the children running, bouncing balls, playing games, doing flips, singing, and dancing. It was better than Pinocchio had imagined!

Every day was play day in Toyland. There
was no school, no teachers, no homework.

"Thank you, Lampwick," Pinocchio said
over and over.

"This is the life!" said Lampwick.

Happy, fun-filled days turned into
happy, fun-filled weeks until one morning,
Pinocchio woke up to a bad surprise.

CHAPTER THIRTY-TWO

DONKEYS

PINOCCHIO yawned and scratched his head. Something had sprouted in the night! He felt around with both hands. He had tall, furry ears!

Jamming his nightcap over his ears, Pinocchio ran and knocked on Lampwick's door.

"I'm sick!" Lampwick called.

"Earache?" called Pinocchio.

"Why, yes," called Lampwick.

"Both ears?" called Pinocchio.

"Yes!" Lampwick opened the door. He, too, had on a nightcap.

"Show me your ears," said Pinocchio.

"You first," said Lampwick.

"Together on three," said Pinocchio. "One, two, THREE!"

They yanked off their caps.

"You look like a donkey!" cried Lampwick.

"No, *you* do!" cried Pinocchio.

They ran around the room, laughing until Lampwick cried, "I feel sick!" He doubled over.

Pinocchio felt sick, too. He fell forward onto his hands. The boys galloped around the room on all fours.

"You've got hee-haw fur!" cried Lampwick.

"You've got hee-haw hooves!" cried Pinocchio.

As they sprouted tails, someone kicked open the door.

Little Man!

CHAPTER THIRTY-THREE

CIRCUS

LITTLE MAN led the donkeys to market. He sold Lampwick to a farmer. He sold Pinocchio to a circus ringmaster. Little Man went back to Toyland, counting his money.

Pinocchio learned circus tricks, and one day Ringmaster put up a sign:

Presenting THE AMAZING DONKEY PINOCCHIO

That night the circus was packed.
Pinocchio stepped into the ring.

"Trot!" cried Ringmaster. "Gallop!"

Pinocchio trotted and galloped.
Everybody cheered.

He looked up and saw a blue-haired
woman. Around her neck she wore a locket
with a picture of a puppet.

"Blue Fairy!" he cried. "It is I, Pinocchio!"

But all that came out was *Hee-haw!*
Hee-haw!

"Quiet!" Ringmaster hit the donkey's nose. Pinocchio began to cry.

"Pinocchio will jump through a hoop!" announced Ringmaster.

Hardly able to see through his tears, Pinocchio jumped, but he tripped on the hoop and fell. When he got up, he was limping.

Ringmaster pulled Pinocchio off the stage.

The next day, he took the lame donkey to market. For a few nickels, he sold him to a drum maker who wanted his hide.

Drum Maker led the donkey to a cliff overlooking the sea. He hung a heavy stone around his neck and tied a rope to one leg. Then he pushed the donkey off the cliff, and sat down to wait for him to drown.

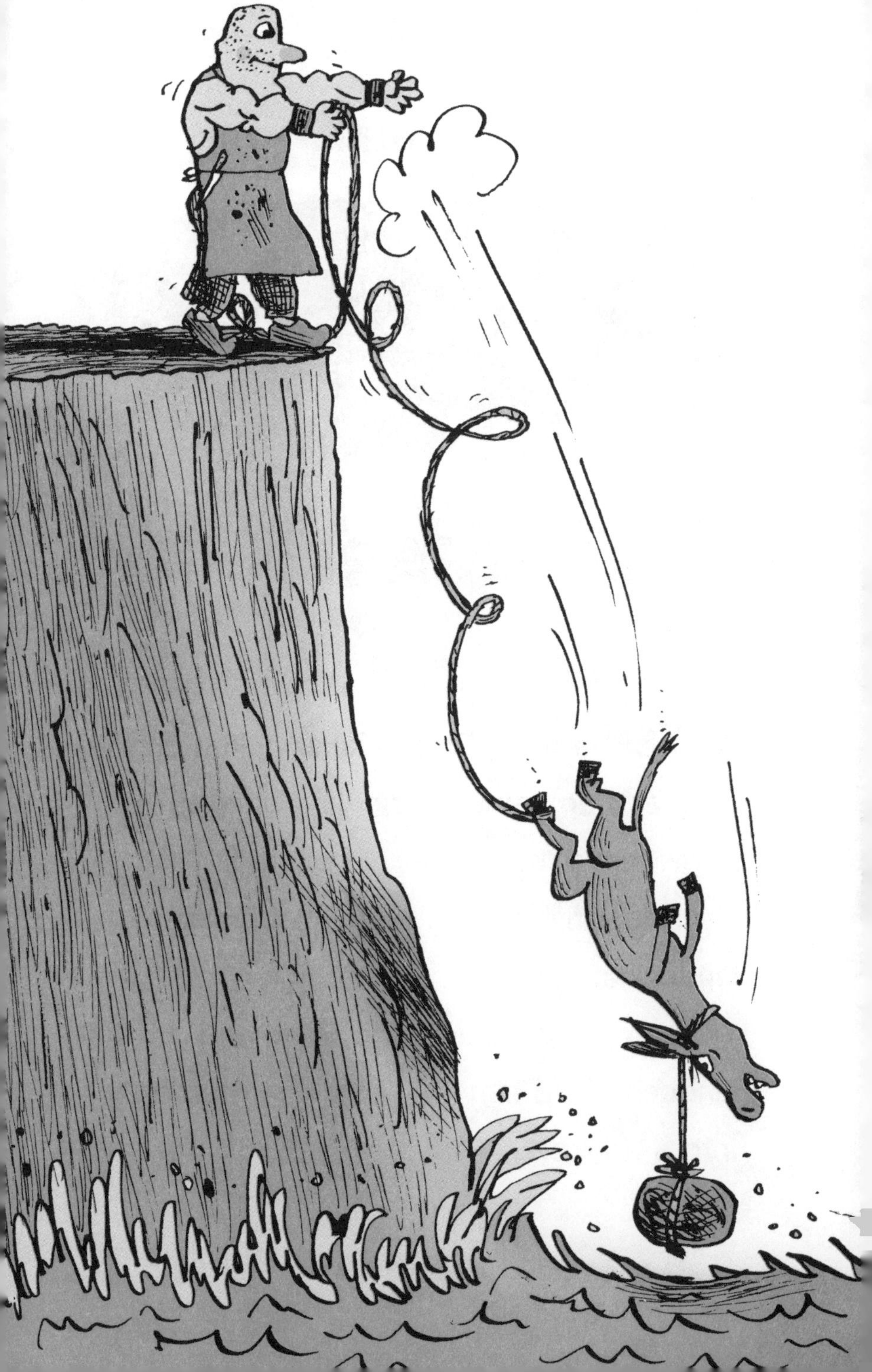

CHAPTER THIRTY-FOUR

SHARK

AFTER a time, Drum Maker pulled on the rope and up came a wriggling puppet!

"Where's my donkey?" he cried.

"Untie my leg and I'll tell you," said Pinocchio.

Drum Maker untied the rope, and Pinocchio told him how he'd been turned into a donkey.

"When you pushed me into the sea," he went on, "Blue Fairy sent a school of fish to eat away the donkey."

Drum Maker glared at Pinocchio. "I'll sell you for firewood!"

"Not today!" cried Pinocchio, and the puppet dove back into the sea.

He swam until he came to a white rock jutting out of the water. On top of the rock stood a goat with blue hair.

"Blue Fairy!" cried Pinocchio. As he swam toward the goat, he felt something swimming up behind him.

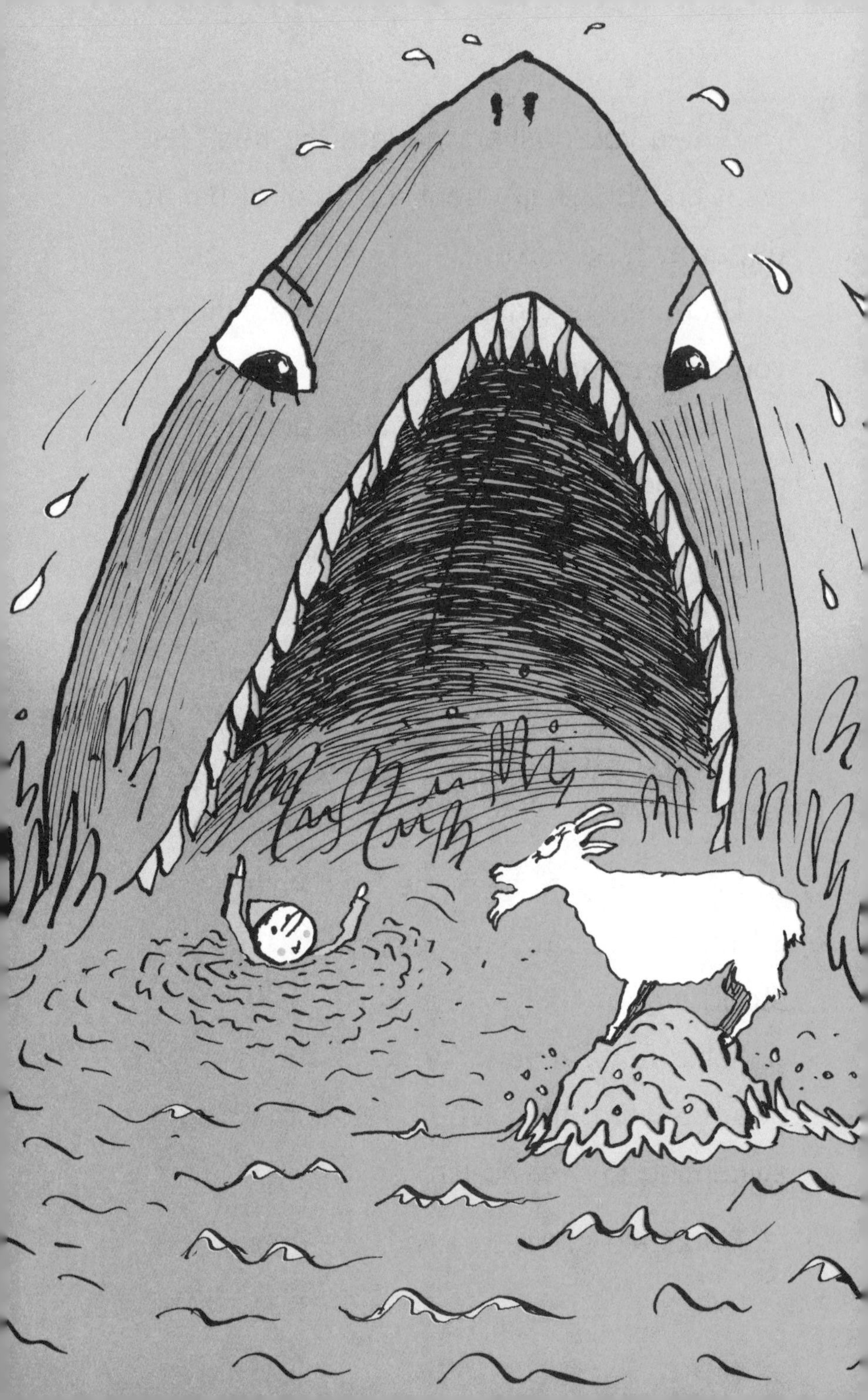

GULP!

Pinocchio squinted in the dark. He saw that the shark had swallowed a tuna, too.

"The shark will soon digest us," said Tuna.

"I don't want to be digested!" cried Pinocchio. He saw a tiny light far down in the shark's belly. "What's that?"

"You go see," said Tuna. "I'll wait here to be digested."

Pinocchio started toward the light.

CHAPTER THIRTY-FIVE

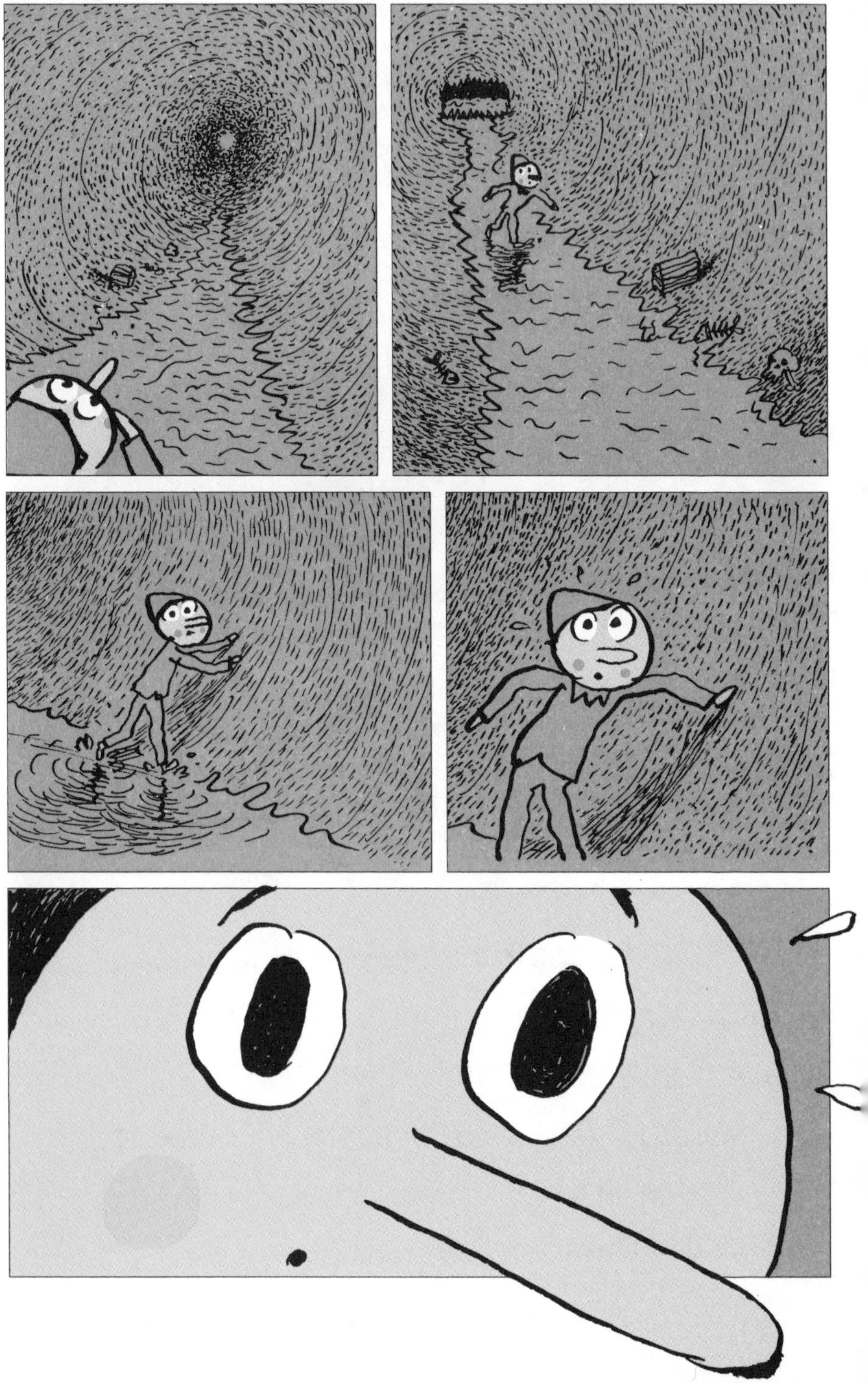

SURPRISE!

PINOCCHIO hopped from puddle to puddle inside the monster's belly. Soon he saw that the light came from a candle on a table. At the table sat an old man.

The puppet gasped. He ran closer and threw his arms around him.

"Daddy!" he cried. "I've found you!"

Geppetto's eyes opened wide. "My dear Pinocchio!" he said.

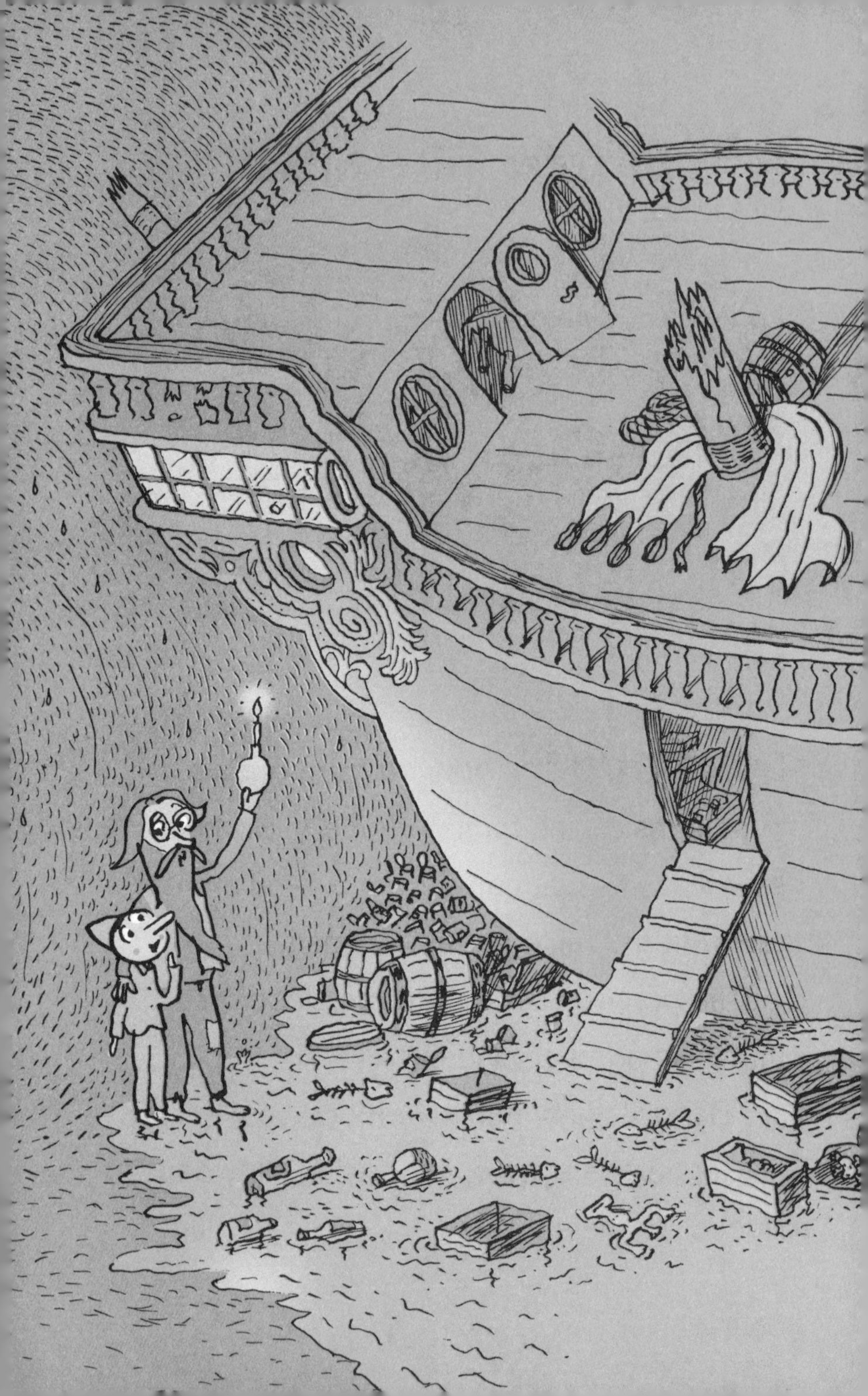

Pinocchio told his daddy how he'd spied him in his little boat.

"I saw you, too," said Geppetto. "Then a huge wave swamped my boat and the giant shark swallowed me. The shark swallowed a cargo ship filled with food and wine, too, so I have eaten well. But now the food is gone and this is my last candle."

"We must escape and swim to shore," said Pinocchio.

Geppetto shook his head. "I can't swim," he said.

"Then I will carry you on my back," said Pinocchio.

"I'm too heavy for you, little puppet," said Geppetto.

Pinocchio picked up the candle, took his daddy's hand, and led him through the shark's belly toward his mouth.

When they reached the end of his throat,
they heard . . .

AH . . . AH . . . AH . . . CHOO!

The shark's sneeze flung them back
into his belly. The candle went out. It was
pitch-dark.

"It's no use," said Geppetto.

"We must try again!" said Pinocchio.
Through the dark, he led the way back. As
they started across the shark's tongue, they
heard a deep rumbling. The shark had fallen
asleep and was snoring with his mouth open.

"Hold on to my back," whispered
Pinocchio.

Geppetto held on and the puppet dove
into the sea.

CHAPTER THIRTY-SIX

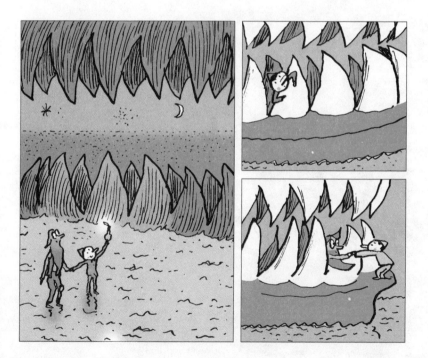

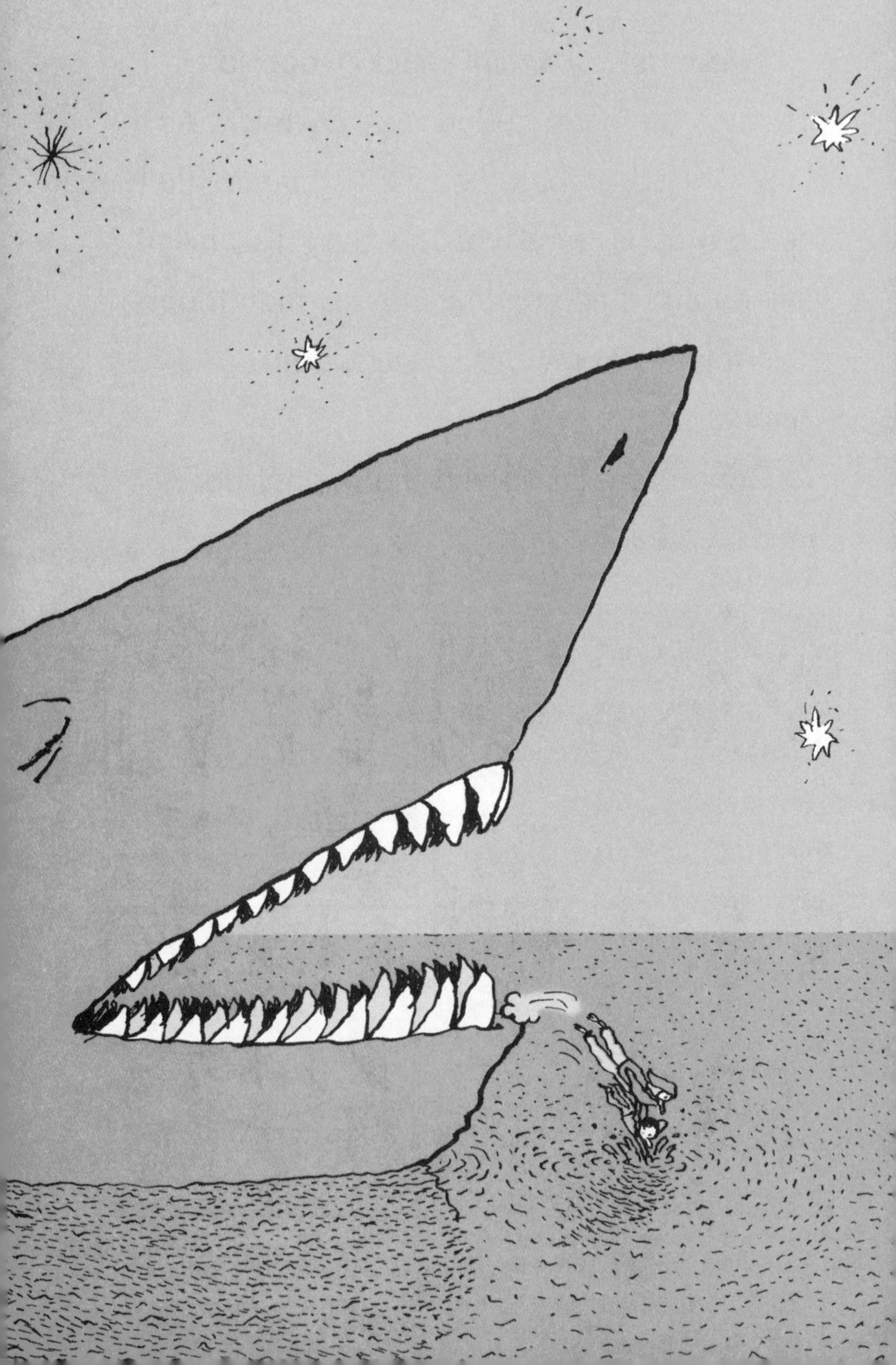

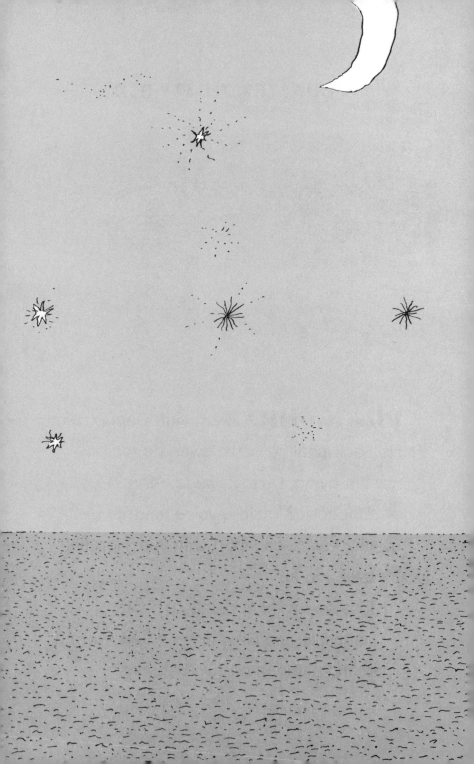

GOOD HEART

PINOCCHIO swam with Geppetto on his back until he could swim no more.

"I'm dying, Daddy!" he cried.

"Pinocchio?" said a voice, and Tuna swam over. "I escaped with you. Hop on! I'll take you in."

Tuna swam them safely to shore.

Pinocchio and Geppetto walked down a road and came upon two beggars.

"Coins?" cried Fox. "I'm so poor, I had to sell my tail for a flyswatter."

"Coins?" cried Cat, holding out his good paw. "I pretended to be blind for so long that now I cannot see!"

"Sorry, we have no coins," said Pinocchio.

Walking on, they came to a hut and went inside.

"Anybody home?" called Pinocchio.

"I am!" called a voice.

Pinocchio looked up. "Cricket!" he cried.

"A goat with blue hair gave me this hut," said Cricket. "You treated me badly, but you are kind to your father, so you may live here."

"Thank you, Cricket!" cried Pinocchio. "Do you know where I can get some milk for my father?"

"From a farmer up the road," said Cricket.

Pinocchio hurried to the farm and asked for a glass of milk.

"It costs a nickel," said the farmer. "If you haven't got a nickel, you can turn my donkey wheel, which draws water for my crops. My donkey used to do it, but he is ill."

"May I see him?" asked Pinocchio. He went to the donkey's stall and found Lampwick taking his last breath. Pinocchio shed tears for his old friend.

Then the farmer led the puppet to the
donkey wheel. He had to bring up one
hundred buckets of water to earn one
glass of milk.

Every day Pinocchio worked on the
donkey wheel to earn milk for his father.

He wove baskets, too, which he sold at the market.

One morning as Pinocchio got dressed, he saw that his clothes were rags. He put his extra nickels into his pocket and started for town to buy new clothes. Who should he meet on his way but Snail.

"Snail!" Pinocchio said. "How is my dear Blue Fairy?"

"She has fallen on hard times," said Snail.

"Buy her food!" cried Pinocchio. He gave Snail all his nickels. "Come back next week for more. Hurry!"

For once, Snail raced off.

Now Pinocchio began working twice as many hours on the donkey wheel. He wove twice the number of baskets.

One night he fell into bed, and in a dream he saw Blue Fairy.

"Pinocchio," she said. "You have a good heart."

Pinocchio woke up. He jumped out of bed ready to go to work, but he looked around, amazed. The walls of the hut were now the walls of a proper house. On the bed lay fine clothes. He put them on, and in the pocket he found a coin purse with a message on it:

Here are your nickels, Pinocchio.
Love
Blue Fairy

But when Pinocchio opened the purse, it was filled with gold coins.

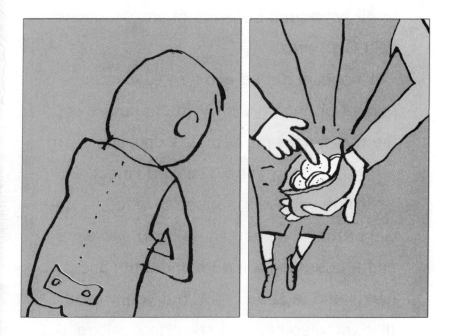

Pinocchio passed a mirror and stopped. Who was this boy staring at him? This fine-looking brown-haired, blue-eyed boy?

Pinocchio ran to the next room, and there was Geppetto, happy and healthy and working with his tools, making a picture frame.

"How did all this happen?" cried Pinocchio.

"It happened because of you, Pinocchio," said Geppetto.

Pinocchio turned and saw a wooden puppet sitting on a chair in the corner of the room, its arms and legs dangling down.

"Was I that puppet?" asked Pinocchio.

"Once you were a piece of wood," said Geppetto. "I carved you a head and eyes and a nose and a mouth and arms and hands and legs and feet. But you proved that you also have a heart, Pinocchio, and so today, you are a boy!"

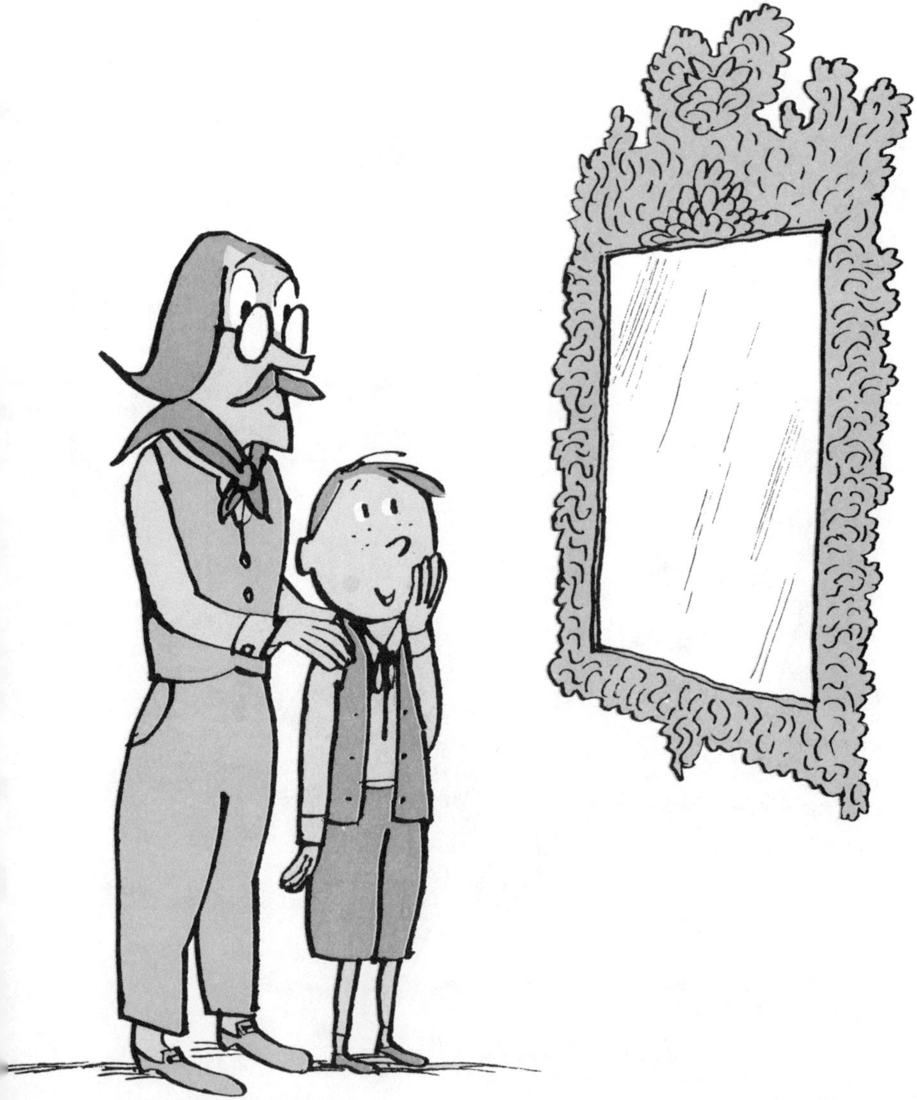

THE END

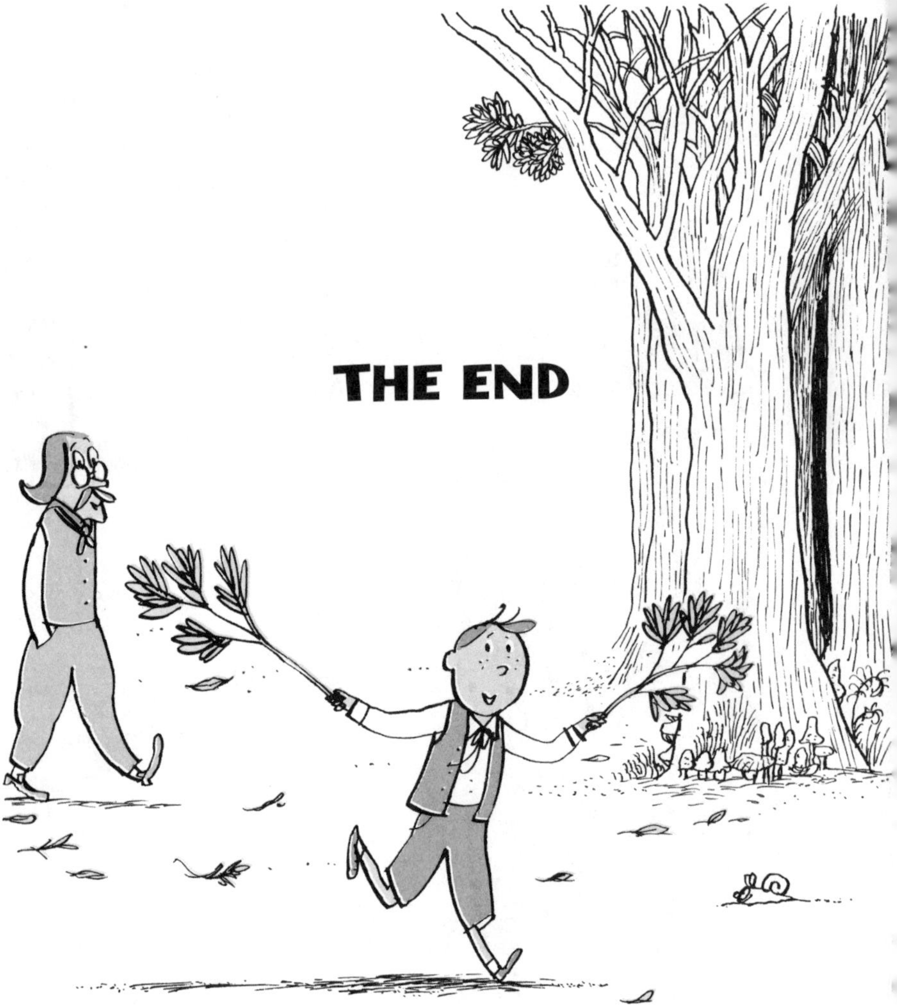